MW01125675

RATTLESNAKE

KISSES

ROBERT FORD AND JOHN BODEN

Published by Apokrupha

copyright, 2019
ISBN: 9781077097940
Cover by Whutta Design
Copy Editing by Kyle Lybeck

apokrupha.com

For Dallas Mayr,
a friend fallen but not far away.

It takes all sorts of people to make the underworld.

—Don Marquis

Don't mistake my kindness for weakness. I'm kind to everyone, but when someone is unkind to me, weak is not what you are going to remember about me.

—Al Capone

CHAPTER ONE

The woman's hands were like featherless birds. They flitted and bounced around the boy's ankle with a palsied precision. The nylon cord wrapped around his thin ankle once, twice, and then a third time before its path led to the cinderblock. The boy was cold and shivered, the breeze from the river reached up over the edge of the bridge and stroked him to goose bumps through his thin T-shirt.

"Mama?" His voice was a small thing in a big empty, too minor to carry an echo.

"It's okay, son." The woman gasped. Her lips were raw livid things on a skull, ravaged white. Her eyes were hiding as far back as possible in dark caves. Water flowed from them freely. She looked at the child and tried to smile but it was broken.

"This is the plan. His plan. I'll be right behind you and we'll be together and happy forever. We shall be warm and safe in the hands of God."

She cocked her head and he saw, again, the bruises on her face. The scab that lived at the corner of her mouth. The purple storm cloud that marred her cheek. Her bony fingers worried over the knot she was making.

"Will I have friends there?" He leaned to fret at the rope around his ankle, tight and itching the skin there.

"So many, Sunshine. More than you can count." She pulled the knot tighter and stood up, her back making tiny popping sounds as she did so. She laid a hand on his head and stroked his hair with the thumb.

"I can count pretty high." The boy beamed and looked up at his mother. The sun was in his eyes and her face was just a blinding glow.

"I know, Pumpkin." She paused and drew a quick and deep breath, kneeling down to resume her task. "You're so very smart."

She finished weaving the rope through the hole in the cinderblock and tied it into another cumbersome knot. She picked up the heavy brick and sat it on the edge of the bridge. She then picked up the boy and sat beside him on the moss-slick railing. She looked at him and ruffled his dark hair. Her lips shook as though she were choking, choking on all the things she wanted to say but instead chose to swallow. Her eyes were frightened rabbits.

"Mama?"

"Yes, son."

"Will you smile when we get there?"

"Oh honey, it's all I'll be able to do." She leaned forward and kissed his forehead.

He smiled and looked into her eyes.

And then she pushed him off.

Chapter Two

The man sat up rail-straight from his slumber. His long-but-thinning hair stuck to his head and neck with thick sweat—the kind usually reserved for delusionary fevers and deathbeds. He ran a shaking hand over his head and then wiped the moisture on his pillow. He sat quietly for a moment before he decided to let the tears roll free.

He slowly lifted his left leg and ran trembling fingers over the deep scar around his ankle. If he closed his eyes, he could still feel the rope. He cried in the dark and his throat felt as though it were full of river water again. He was about to lie back down when the phone rang. He picked it up before it screamed a second time.

"Yes." He croaked, swallowing back the tears.

"Dallas?" A voice asked, timidly.

"Texas or TV show?"

"Um...TV show." The voice on the other end of the line was swaddled in uncertainty.

"Season premiere reached 10K. No pets, no kids."

"Well, it's my mist—"

Dallas interrupted. "Nope. Not the right channel, man. *Mystery* is on another one. We need to get cable for that kind of show. You dig?" He tried hard to mask the annoyance in his rusty voice. His lungs were crying for a cigarette.

There was a pause, pregnant to the point of dilation.

"I think. Yes. This one. It's playing at the Elks Club Lodge. They run great movies there. There's a show at midnight tomorrow." More silence.

"I'll bring my kid and we'll meet you there."

"Okay. I'll wear my blue jacket."

"Have the popcorn." Dallas said as he put the phone back on its cradle.

He lay back down and stared into the dark pool of the ceiling. It was like that place in the river where the shallows met the deep holes at night. If he stared long enough he could see his mother floating there. Her hair, a soft halo full of branches and fish. He often wondered if she were in the hands of God, until he remembered he wasn't a believer. He reached out and grabbed the pack of cigarettes from the nightstand. Instead of sleeping, he lay there smoking until the sun came up.

CHAPTER THREE

The smoother than caramel tones of Otis Redding filled the interior of the car.

Dallas reached over and adjusted the volume knob ever so slightly, turning it up. "I love Marvin Gaye."

The Kid slowly turned his head to stare. His mouth was open in shock. "You're fuckin' kiddin' me, right? This *ain't* Marvin Gaye."

Dallas watched the boy as his face grew redder, his lips tightening and threatening to disappear altogether. He counted another beat or two in his head.

"I know that. It's Sam Cooke. And how many goddamn times do I have to tell you not to say ain't?" Dallas boomed, barely able to keep the corner of his mouth from turning up in an attempted smile.

"It's Otis *Reddddinnnng.*" The Kid drew out the last name, as if speaking to a toddler. "How can you *possibly* mix him up with Marvin Gaye or Sam fucking Cooke! Why not throw in Al Green or Teddy Pendergrass while you're at it!"

Dallas grunted and turned his attention back to the entrance of the Elks Club. He knew damned well it was Otis Redding. He'd been listening to the man before the Kid was a pimple on his father's ass. Truth be told, he usually did shit like that just to get under the Kid's skin. But right now, it was because he needed to focus on the task at hand, and it gave the Kid something to ramble on about instead of screwing with the seat switches or the car windows, or pushing every visible button in the car like a bored three-year-old. He stole a sideways glance at the young man in the passenger seat. He was sitting there, his lips going full tilt. He was doing the alphabet again. Two men stumbled out of the Elks. Both heavyset. One wearing a red and black flannel, the other a denim work shirt. They made their way to a rusted Chevy pickup with a rebel flag plastered on the rear window and started it up. The engine coughed out smoke but held steady and they left the gravel lot. Their right taillight was out.

Dallas checked his watch and lit a cigarette, distantly hearing the Kid prattle on about Stax Records, he was doing record labels apparently. He let the smoke fill his mouth and then parted his lips slightly to give it an escape. It fled up and over his face, making him squint as he looked at his wrist. It was seven minutes 'til.

It was always like this on an unknown request. Tense. Senses heightened. Not exactly... *fearful*, but cautious. In the old days, it was easier. Still had to be careful, but you meet the prospective client, work out the details, complete the job and move on with your life. But these days? Shit. One wrong move and you end up on a goddamn *Dateline* news segment. Worse yet, you fuck it up and you end up *going viral.*

A too-thin blonde wearing a plaid shirt tied into a halter-top stepped outside the Elks building and took an unsteady step in her cowboy boots. She leaned over and pulled her hair back in a practiced move, and Dallas watched her throw up into the juniper bushes. She shook her head and spit a few times, then moved toward the wall. A small glimpse of flame and Dallas watched her draw on a cigarette, resting her head against the cool brick wall. She hawked and spit again, tossed the smoke on the ground and went back inside. She apparently had more money to earn.

Dallas realized the mosquito drone of the Kid had paused and the sound of a belt being undone and the rumble strip pull of a zipper brought his attention back to the car.

"The fuck do you think you're doin'?"

"Gotta take a leak. We're on a stakeout. I was trying to be, y' know... inconspicuous."

Dallas lifted his forearm to his nose and sniffed.

"Dallas, what're you–"

"Nope. I don't smell like bacon. You smell like bacon? We're not the goddamn heat and we're not on a stakeout. We're *obserrrrrvinnng*. That means watching and making notes in your head. So, let me break it down for you. You whip that limp noodle out in my vehicle and get piss on my seat and I'll kill you myself, your uncle Skeeter be damned." He took a drag off his cigarette and let it out slowly, allowing his point to sink in.

The Kid shook his head and zipped up. "All right, all right. Fuck's sakes. You forget to drink your Metamucil this morning or something?" He opened the door and skulked off into the shadows.

Dallas turned his head and let out a breath. It was almost midnight. No sign of anything off kilter or out of place. No strange looking too-clean cars parked in the shadows. Nothing to make the hair stand on the back of his neck. Things felt okay or at least as okay as they could be with the Kid along.

The car door opened and the Kid slid back into the passenger seat.

"Shake it more than once, you're playing with it."

"At least I can still get it up, ol' man."

"That's what your sister tells me."

"Oh, fuck you."

A man in charcoal gray pants and a blue jacket stepped around the far side of the building. Medium build with a healthy paunch starting to take shape. He carried a black duffel bag in his right hand. He paused at the entrance and scanned the parking lot for a moment, then stepped inside. He was all nerves and it was obvious from ten yards away.

"Bingo." Dallas sighed and dropped his cigarette into the cup on the dashboard. It made a small hiss as it met the dregs of the morning's coffee.

"When we're inside, shut your mouth and listen. Keep your eyes on your surroundings. You're not here to check out the asses on the barmaids. You aren't here to wax prophetic about what the sticky shit on the floor might be or how it got there. You're here to make sure nothing and no one unusual sneaks up on us. If shit goes sideways, follow my lead, got it?"

"Yeah, I got it."

Dallas kept his stony gaze leveled at the boy.

"I said I got it. Sheesh!"

They stepped from the car and headed toward the Elks and the prospect waiting inside.

CHAPTER FOUR

Decades ago, the building had started out as a movie theatre. The L-shaped foyer had a nice little snack shop and café. In the seventies, they had tried their hand at adult films and then the Elks took over and transformed the café into a small bar. Porn gave way to hipsters jonesing for classic films running in small theatres, and the Elks took up a spear and joined the battalion. At a small table beneath a curling poster for the movie *Southern Comfort*, the men sat.

"This okay to do here?" The man asked, and stole what was easily his thirtieth glance around the foyer.

"Will be if you stop acting like a priest who just got done playing Little Jack Horner with a choirboy. Stop gawping around." Dallas spoke sternly but his voice never rose in volume. The hard edge came from those eyes of his. Dallas took a sip of his drink and winced. He wasn't much of a soda fan to begin with but this shit was ghastly. Barely any fizz and the mix was uneven. He looked at the squirrelly man across the table and spoke.

"I know what you need. Nobody calls me for anything else." Dallas glanced at the bar where a buxom woman handed a bucket of popcorn to a young man with a ridiculous beard.

"You come highly recommended."

"Doesn't anyone who does something for you that you don't

want to do yourself?" Dallas wished he had a smoke. Wished you could still smoke in these places. Hell, there was a time when you could smoke in the goddamn hospital. The doctor would have a fucking Pall Mall hanging from his lip while he read your fucking X-ray. Dallas pinched his thigh under the table to yank his own leash away from a nicotine fit.

Dallas took a sip from his drink and nodded at the man. "You know the price. If you're good with that, all we need is a name and address and maybe a small list of other places if they're not home when we call." There was movement in his periphery as the Kid nodded enthusiastically. His eyes were shining and he was doing that thing with his hands, clenched to near fists as he rubbed the fingertips against the palm of his hands. Dallas held up a finger to the man and leaned over in the Kid's direction.

"Why don't you go check on the car?"

The Kid looked at him, almost wounded. "But I want to stay..."

"Go walk around a few minutes. You're getting away. Go pull it tight—do an alphabet. Go with alphabet new wave. Come back when you're done." He patted the young man's cheek and the Kid stood and shook his head. He began to speak at a normal volume as he headed for the door:

"A is for ABC, sang *Poison Arrow*, B is for Berlin, sang *The Metro*." The door closed before they could hear the letter C.

Dallas returned his attention to the man across from him. "The Kid is okay. He's just an odd one."

"Asperger's, looks like. Gotta nephew is a Burger. Spooky little fucker. The housewife magazines call 'em Aspies but I think that sounds like some annoying kind of dog and these are kids." The man smiled. "My wife and I call 'em Burgers and then we ascribe them different names that go with the level of their Aspergeriness." He took a swig of his flat 7-Up. "I'd say your kid there is a Big Mac." He chuckled.

Dallas did not. He stared until the man's smile suffocated beneath its weight and then leaned in. "P.O. Box 3. In town. The list of requested information. We don't get it in three days, we don't do it. But we keep the popcorn. It keeps our mouths too full to talk. Am I clear?"

"Crystal." The man stole another look around and stood. Before he could step away, Dallas laid a thin but strong hand on his forearm, the one holding the duffel bag.

"Leave the popcorn. I trust it's all there?"

"It is." The man held the bag out for Dallas to accept.

"One more thing. You make fun of the Kid again or disrespect him or any others by calling them fucking fast food... I'll take you out for nothing." He never took his eyes off the man's face. When it began to shake slightly, he cemented the fear. "And I'll make it very unpleasant." Dallas dropped a smile and a wink. "Am I...?"

"Crystal." The man whispered, a voice that squeaked like an old hinge, pulled away, and disappeared into the theatre.

Dallas finished his drink and went outside.

CHAPTER FIVE

"V is for Visage. Sang *Mind Of A Toy*. W is for Wang Chung. Sang *Dance Hall Days*. I hate that *Everybody Have Fun Tonight* song. The rest of that album was good though." The Kid inhaled and let it out slowly. His fists were loosening up and he wasn't pressing his fingernails into the palms of his hands as sharply.

A flicker of movement in the gravel caught his eye and he squatted down. A small brown toad hopped toward the darker shadows of a steel drum. He reached out and picked up the toad, smiling as it wriggled in his hands. Its skin was smooth and cool but not moist. The Kid held it up in the dim lights of the Elks parking lot. The toad blinked and puffed its throat out. "X is for... XTC. Sang *Making Plans For Nigel*." The toad pulled a foreleg free and rested its stubby fingers on the Kid's thumb.

Chesterfield Rheingold Williams is the Kid's given name.

His mother thought it would be a real hoot to name him after shitty cigarettes and shittier beer and by the time the Kid got to the school playground, it was a real hoot 'n hollerin knee slapper of a joke. Not more than a day or two went by without singsong chants of Chester the Molester, even though most of the dirty heathens calling him that had no idea what it meant. Once in a while, the name-calling wasn't enough to slake their thirst and the Kid walked home with a busted lip or torn shirt.

12

His mother never bothered to see any of it. He was as important as a living room ashtray—a flea market knick-knack to glance at once in a while and notice without admiration. Her boyfriend Darrell didn't help things. If it were up to him, the boy's name would have been legally changed to "fuckin' retard."

The Kid kept to himself and ignored their insults, though most of the time they pretended he didn't exist. The Kid went inward instead of striking out—exploring the woods beyond the Briarwood Estates trailer park. They weren't a part of that park, per se, choosing instead to plant their rusted out of style shitbox about a quarter-mile down the road from it, pariah-like.

The moss-covered logs and thin trickles of streams in the woods became his safe haven. He found things in the woods—sun-bleached deer antlers or the milky shed skin of snakes. He played with the crawfish from the stream sometimes—sometimes it was with a magnifying glass or pliers. He still wasn't sure if he had imagined it or not, but sometimes he thought he could hear the softest little squeaky noises coming from them when he took off one of their legs. Oh how they flapped their tails in his hand. It somehow quieted things inside him. It made the words of the kids at school fade away to a low hum like radio static on a far away station. That blissful hiss.

Sometimes, he would imagine himself on a saloon stage playing music like his daddy. Momma had never said anything at all about him, and the Kid had never actually met his father in real life, but he knew better. No way he could love music as much as he did without it being ribboned right into his DNA.

He thought of his daddy sometimes. Hair slicked back. Scuffed, but well-loved, cowboy boots on—black and dirty. Weathered 12-string guitar with a *wide black strap around his neck and shoulders, as he flirted with the waitresses and sang about heartache and loss to the crowd. Living life on the highway, as carefree as a rambling rose. Cool as rain in September.*

The thought always made the Kid smile, but also a little sad. He knew what it was like to want a dream, and he didn't blame his daddy for going after it. He just wished he would call or write from time to time—a birthday card or something—maybe a postcard reading about life on the road.

Darlene, his older sister, heard from her daddy about once every two months or so—sometimes a phone call, other times a post card or short letter. And around her birthday, Darlene would get a small box of Whitman's Sampler chocolates from him. Same kind. Same size. Every year. But hey, it was something.

Darlene claimed first pick of the candy, but she always shared with the Kid and he made sure to always thank her for it. She was good like that. When she held the box out for him to pick a chocolate, she always had a smile but a sad expression on her face. He knew she felt a little sorry for him but it was all right.

Wasn't until later in life that Darlene's expression changed to fear and uncertainty when she looked at him. By then, he couldn't really blame her, but he would never hurt a hair on her head. No reason to—Darlene had never hurt him in his life.

Not like Momma's boyfriend Darrell. That man deserved every damned thing he got. Every. Last. Thing. And then maybe a second helping.

The door to the Elks swung open on springs in need of some oil. The Kid's gaze swung up and he saw the man from the meeting step free from the doorway. The man looked left and right, then walked around the far side of the building, off into the darkness. Seconds later, Dallas stepped beneath the red neon sign and into the gravel lot. The cherry on his cigarette glowed like a demonic third eye.

The Kid looked down at the feel of a wet paper towel in his hand. The toad's mouth was open wide and even in the dim light, the Kid could see its tongue, glistening and pink as freshly chewed bubble gum. Its eyes bulged beyond their sockets and the Kid opened his hand, and saw the innards had burst from its small body onto his palm. He slung it into the weeds along the side of the lot and splashed his hand into a gray puddle of water. The chips of rock felt rough beneath his hand, and he scrubbed it along the water's bottom, before wiping it on his jacket.

He was feeling better. Not so fluttery and tight inside anymore. "Y is for... the Yachts. Sang *Suffice to Say.*" He bit the inside of his lip. "Fuck Z." He started to stand and got maybe three steps before he stopped and closed his eyes tight. "Z is for Zwischenfall. Sang *Sandy Eyes.*" He opened his eyes and exhaled slowly. A thin smile scurried across his lips like an insect. He started to mumble to himself, fairly audible. "I'm pretty goddamn sure I'm the only person in this state who knows about that band. They were a great electronic group."

Dallas put the duffel on the floor in the back of the car and lit a cigarette. He slapped a hand on the roof of the car once to get the Kid's attention: "Come along, grasshopper."

"What's that mean?"

They both slid into the car seats and Dallas started the engine. "Grasshopper? *Kung fu?* TV show with David Carradine. Snatch the pebble from my hand and all that shit." Dallas rolled his window down. "You got nothing? Clearly I am failing in my teaching. After this job's over, we're grabbing a couple of icy six-packs and we're gonna unfuck that. You've got to see *Kung fu.*"

The Kid smiled. "You're not failing. I think you're doing pretty good." He took on a slightly pensive look for a moment.

"David Carradine was in the *Kill Bill* movies and hung himself while whacking it in Thailand."

"Mmmmhmmmm." Dallas gave a hint of a smile and nodded. "Well, now we wait. Three days to give us the details or else we've got an easy payday."

"That ever happen?"

"Not too damned often. If they've got enough sand in their shorts to bring a bag of money and meet face to face, most people have their mind made up. This guy's serious. Now we just keep checking the P.O. box."

"Then it's show time?"

Dallas took a last puff from his cigarette and flicked it outside. "Then it's show time."

The Kid gave one last glance at where he had thrown the toad's body before they pulled out of the lot. He kept his face to the window so Dallas couldn't see the remorseful expression he wore.

CHAPTER SIX

The lot behind the Elks had emptied over an hour ago, all but the one vehicle nearest the gulley that butted the marsh. Morris sat in his wife's Lexus and watched the droplets of sweat fall from his forehead and land on the steering wheel. He had the window down and the breeze was cool but humid. The air was heavy with the sound of crickets and peep frogs.

He rubbed his fingers against his closed eyes and sighed heavily. "You're locked in now, buddy boy." He sat up straight and wiped his brow on the sleeve of his jacket. Raising his arm, just slightly, was enough to allow his own sour smell to escape. He looked over to the passenger seat, to the pile of *Home* magazines and gardening catalogs there. He frowned at her gym towel on the floor and the sugar-free gum wrappers surrounding it. He had taken her car tonight in case he felt his nerve slipping. He knew one glance at this pig-sty-on-wheels would remind him why he needed this bitch gone and not only because she couldn't resist riding pole every chance that presented itself. He knew she was a whore going in. Hell, he'd gotten a knob polish on their first date that was so good he thought he was going to have to dig out the needle nosed pliers to get his underwear out of his asshole. He felt a smile start to grow and bit his tongue to kill it.

He picked up the magazine on the top of the pile and flipped it over. Across the top of the back cover advertisement was a phone number and the name Chad. He grimaced as bile raced up his throat and coated his back teeth. He knew that was the guy she was spreading for. He was going to have her gone before she asked him for a divorce though. No way he was giving that bitch any of his shit. She would get exactly half of shit—which is shit. He laughed and it came out more like a bark. Outside the car, something ran through the high grass and plopped into the water. Morris sat there and shut his eyes again.

Behind his closed lids, his wife died a million deaths and his mistress took her throne, and all of his earthly treasures remained his own.

CHAPTER SEVEN

Victoria Rose let out a long, satisfied sigh and trailed her fingers ever so lightly over her sweat-glazed breasts. Her thighs were still trembling. She turned her head to watch Chad standing at the sink, running a washcloth over himself. His body was a work of art, thick already by his genes alone, but muscled from days of hard labor as a roofer. The mat of fine hair on his chest glistened and Victoria bit her lip, wondering if she had time for a round two.

He caught her watching him and grinned. "Them's some awful dirty thoughts running through your head." He tossed the wet rag on the bathroom counter and walked back to the bed, lying on his stomach beside her. "And here I thought I did a good job of satisfying you."

"Oh, you most definitely did. But it's like great wine. Can you ever *really* have enough?" she purred, a consummate actress.

Chad nuzzled the scruff of his beard against her hip and she squealed out, laughing and pushing his head away from her. "Nononononononononooo!"

He relented and rose from the bed, grabbed his jeans from a jumble on the floor, and started pulling them on. "As much as I'd like to stay, I can't. Got to get to a job up in Medford. Some rich bastard with a restaurant chain wants a new roof on his pool house."

19

He reached for his boots. "You taking a shower before heading out?"

She considered it, then shook her head. "Not today. I have some things to do and I want to know I'm carrying you around inside me all afternoon."

That made him pause and swivel his head toward her. His mouth trapped somewhere between smile and grimace. "That might be the dirtiest thing I've ever heard you say." Chad leaned down and kissed her stomach. His rough fingertips brushed along the inside of her right thigh, grazing against the very core of her and she gasped, breaking the kiss.

"Don't start something you can't finish right now."

Chad snickered and nodded. "Just giving you something to think about when you're out playing with the girls this afternoon and having wine or... whatever." He buckled his belt and pulled a blue T-shirt over his head. "Same time on Thursday?"

"Not sure yet, but I'll text you."

He leaned down and kissed her again. "Gotta run. Lock up when you leave."

Victoria heard the door open and close, and she let out another exhale of satisfaction before she sat up on the edge of the bed and looked around. Chad's apartment was small and oddly decorated.

No, that wasn't right. Not oddly decorated, but *simply. Sparsely. Well,* she thought, Chad *wasn't exactly part of a think tank.* She knew he was nothing but a toy to play with for a while, and he probably knew as well. She hoped so at least. And why shouldn't she have her own toys to play with from time to time? Morris damn well did. She knew when she married him he was a player—hell, she was no saint back then either—but a part of her thought maybe marriage was enough to tame them both.

She was wrong.

There was the redheaded stripper with the tattoos and piercings. Then, Morris had a very short-lived fling with the Filipino cleaning woman at the office. Tiny little thing she was, and Victoria just bet Morris spun her like a top when he had her in bed.

The brunette intern with the freckles and the huge knockers. Another redhead from who the hell knows where. Buxom. Ol' Morris had a type all right—a full shirt and a place to park his little thing.

And after that, Victoria stopped giving a shit or keeping track.

Hurt turned to anger and anger to indifference and now she felt... she turned it over in her mind to figure out the right word. *Entitled*. No. Not that. *Justified!* That was it! She felt JUSTIFIED in her plans.

Victoria wasn't the kind of woman to give notice or warnings on items of common knowledge. Morris knew better, but he chose to ignore his knowledge and act with his little head instead of his big one. There would be no warnings for the man she married. Only action.

She sat down on Chad's couch and lit a cigarette, leaned back against the rough cloth and watched the smoke rise in milky spirals. She stared at the rusty tie-dye of water stain on the ceiling. Victoria smiled and nodded to herself, then stubbed out the cigarette. She reached for her purse and withdrew her phone and a pack of matches with a number scrawled on the inside flap. Victoria stared at the handwritten number for a moment, considering.

It was time to move on to better things and enjoy the financial fruits of Morris' hard work. Morris had been fun for a while, but this lifestyle had grown tiresome. As a toy, he had long since bored her.

It was time to be done with this particular ball of yarn.

CHAPTER EIGHT

Dallas had dropped the Kid at his trailer and driven the six miles home. He was sitting on the back porch and watching the stars as they winked. He shook his glass slightly to hear the ice cubes rattle and then took a small swig of the Scotch it held. He had a radio playing softly in the window. He sucked the final bit of life from his Winston and then flicked it into the yard. Dallas closed his eyes and listened to the night—crickets and peeps and the almost invisible sound of Creedence Clearwater Revival on the radio, along with his own rasping breath.

First meetings with a new client were always tense but he was beginning to relax now that it was over. His tight muscles loosened and Dallas began to feel calmed and warm. His lips began to curl upward into a smile. He was within sight of Zen when he heard the bastard phone ringing in the house. Dallas opened his eyes and sat upright. It rang again. "Every fucking time." He sighed.

"Yes," he said, as he put the phone to his ear.

"Is this Dallas?" The voice was thick and sultry and he wagered if he could taste it, it would be worth savoring.

"Texas or TV?"

"What?"

Dallas could almost hear the question mark. His only reply was a very deep sigh, the breath whistling slightly as it fled through his teeth.

"I think Texas." The woman on the other end sounded confused but not nervous.

"Great vacation spot. Not for Kids or animals though."

"Expensive?" She asked, a bounce of confidence in her tone as she picked up on what was going down.

"I think you can get away for ten days at $5000."

"When do we leave?"

"We can discuss the travel plans tomorrow night. Battastelli's."

"I know the place."

"Fine. Nine o'clock. Bring the brochures." He dropped the receiver into its cradle and stood there for a minute. He contemplated going back outside to reach for his moment of Zen once more but decided against it. Instead, Dallas sat on his recliner and turned on the television. After a few channels he found one running *Little Big Man*. It made him think of his dad. Long before that man had been driven to yank stakes and pull a Houdini-level disappearing act by his whackadoo mother. So many lazy Saturday afternoons lying on the living room floor, watching that and other westerns with him. He left it on but was asleep within twenty minutes.

CHAPTER NINE

The best time to go to the post office was about a half hour after opening. Dallas had learned this —like most things in his life—by being quiet and watching. There was always a flurry of people as the doors opened up but after they left, checking a box off their "to do" list for the day, crowds didn't appear again until just before noon.

Dallas stepped inside and took a hard left, then a right to where his P.O. box awaited. He gave a casual glance around and then squatted to unlock the box. Nestled inside was a large manila envelope folded in half. Dallas withdrew it and tucked it inside his jacket, then locked the box again.

Even now, after all this time, the sight of a new envelope—a new job—made his heart beat a little faster. The challenge of what was to come. Studying the details of the target. The routines. Making sense of life's patterns and searching for a weakness to properly assess the job. It was all about the right approach.

In many ways, it was solving a puzzle, and puzzles were one thing Dallas had always enjoyed. They taught you patience. It kept the mind sharp, when you turned things over this way and that. Though he had never solved that damned Rubik's Cube. Goddamned thing was from Satan himself.

Dallas walked through the parking lot and slid into the driver's seat of his car. The Kid had an excited expression painted on his face.

"Well? Easy payday or not?"

Dallas leaned back against the leather cushion. "Which would make you happier? Having the job and getting paid, or just getting paid without doing a damned thing?"

The Kid opened his mouth and closed it just as quickly. He chewed on his bottom lip, then took a drink from the plastic bottle of root beer he held. "It's not that I'm lazy or nothin'... but I just think it's *always* gonna be better to get paid for not liftin' a damn finger."

Dallas stared at him a moment, then nodded. "Good answer, Kid. This is for the money. It's always for the money, like any other job, and just like any other job, it's okay to take a certain... *pride* in your work. Enjoy it even. To a degree."

Dallas pointed at the Kid. "But you listen up and listen good. You ever start feeling that taking the life of another human being is anythin' at all like happiness to you, like something you look forward to...then it's time to close shop. Go be a carpenter or a garbage man or some shit."

Dallas reached for the center console and shook a Winston free from his pack. He pinched it between his lips and lit it. "Now, I'm not talking about some of the human garbage that comes up from time to time. Some of them get what they damn well deserve. That's different. Like the kiddy diddler I told you about down in Glenville. I'd have done that job for free, but when I did him, it felt good and right. Like I was throwing away a pile of dog shit I ran across on my

26

lawn. But for everyday marks, if that feeling of happiness starts to be a pattern, you're in trouble and it's time to get out."

"All right." The Kid nodded as he listened and took another swig of root beer, then cocked his head and gave a little grin. "But you gonna tell me or what?"

Dallas withdrew the envelope from his jacket. "We've got a job."

The Kid's smile grew wider at the announcement and it wasn't unnoticed by Dallas, but he let it go. He supposed it was only natural the Kid was excited. The boy had his quirks but he wasn't dumb and besides that, the Kid knew when he should shut up and listen most of the time. That alone was an admirable thing.

"We'll lay it all out later and go over the details. Make some choices. There'll be decisions made. I'll tell you why or why not on certain things so you can learn to plan."

"What's his name?" The Kid reached for the envelope and Dallas snatched it back.

"Later."

"Oh *come onnnn*, Dallas! Just his name. Let me have that for now, please?"

The damned Kid really did look like it was Christmas Eve and he was ready to tear into the biggest present under the tree. Dallas chuckled to himself and peeled open the flap of the envelope, pulling out a sheet of thick cotton bond.

"Well I'll be damned."

"What is it, Dallas? C'mon, you're killing me here."

Dallas looked over at him. "I didn't think fussy britches at the

Elk's Lodge had it in him. But the mark isn't a he. It's a she." He turned the paper around so the Kid could read the laser printed name at the top of the page:

VICTORIA ROSE MUSSEY

"A woman?"

"They tend to piss people off too." Dallas took a drag from the Winston. "You all right with that? No children and no pets is the line for *me*. Everybody's got their line."

The Kid glanced through the passenger window, considering it and turned to Dallas, nodding. "I'm all right with it."

The grin had faded on the Kid's face but the gleam of excitement was still in his eyes.

That didn't go unnoticed either.

CHAPTER TEN

The Kid sat in the corner of the trailer's sloping living room, his back against the warped paneling. He looked at his jacket and hat atop a mix of sneakers and boots near the door. There was no light except what trickled in from the pole outside by the curve in the road. He closed his eyes and pretended he heard his Mama and Darrell arguing in the kitchen. He liked to pretend and rewrite his memories so he could leave out the things like the meaty thunder of fist on face or the inevitable hollering of "Yer fucking retard son." The Kid sat and rocked and remembered, sorta.

The Kid was an odd one from the get go. After knowing him just a short while, one could almost envision the sperm that created him pacing around the womb, talking low to itself and casting furtive glances at the egg it sought to get with. He was a loud and fussy baby. His mother already resented him for the enormous splinter he rammed into the foot of her life. The baby wouldn't sleep and cried relentlessly. "Colic" the doctors said.

As he grew, his other quirks revealed themselves. Sensitivity to noises and lights. Inability to maintain eye contact and lack of understanding basic cues in a social situation. The doctors wouldn't officially diagnose him with Asperger's but they definitely placed him on their spectrum and offered to ply him with enough drugs to make a rampaging rhino as docile as a bird-fed cat. Mama chose to spend the money on smokes and booze instead. As he grew older, the Kid learned to soothe himself. He invented the Alphabet trick as a method of calming himself when he felt his spring about to uncoil and pop. His camera mind for details and trivia made it a fun exercise for him to decompress.

Now, a young man of twenty-two, and the Kid could almost pass for normal—so long as you didn't engage with him for too long. Then his eyes jumped nervously and he'd pace or shake his leg. He was smart as hell and knew more about a million things on a myriad of subjects than a million people knew about one thing. He raised himself and did a decent job of it. He was a stand up adult in a world that devoured them like candy.

The Kid had come home from work early. He was making a hard six bucks an hour plucking feathers from dead chickens at the poultry plant on the edge of town. He was cold and damp and smelled bad.

He went in and saw Mama on the couch. She was sleeping. Her mouth was a dam of scab and swelling holding back a thick pool of blood. Her eyes were slightly open. The Kid's heart jumped and he felt his spring uncoil. "Ma?" He started toward her, stopping halfway to turn and pace back toward the door.

"Oh Mama. Oh Shit." This was the mantra he spewed as he paced and got a little closer to the couch with every round. He finally knelt and held a hand to her mouth. No breath kissed his palm. The Kid closed his eyes. He knew he was supposed to cry, but he couldn't. The tears simply wouldn't come. He sat there for nearly an hour before he stood and walked down the

hall. He heard Darrell's drunken animal noises before he even got to their bedroom door.

If only the hammer hadn't made such a mess. But he'd grown so tired. Tired of hearing that man pound and scratch at Darlene's locked door, slurring filthy things about how girl's oughta love their daddies. Tired of hearing the rage-filled meetings of fist and face when Darrell and his Mama fought. He only wanted it all to end. To protect Darlene. Sometimes you have to do bad things to make good things.

Sometimes people don't understand that. Darlene hadn't understood that. He had to watch her affection for him dry up and blow away like so many autumn leaves, carried on the breeze of her screaming.

CHAPTER ELEVEN

Dallas sat at the back most table of Battistelli's. He nursed his second glass of wine as he kept his eyes on the door. It was nearly nine. He had just put his drink down when the door opened and a woman entered. The small smile he had been working up, his work uniform so to speak, withered like a flower after a frost.

"Oh fuck." He sighed under breath as Mrs. Morris Mussey sauntered his way. She was a sight to behold for sure. He stood up and stepped around to the other side of the table and pulled the chair out. "Please." He offered and she smiled, pulling down the material that was trying to pass as a skirt and sat.

"Thank you, Dallas... or is it Mr. Livingston?"

"Doesn't really matter, not my real name anyway." He smiled but it felt flypaper sticky.

The waiter arrived at the table and asked if they were ready to order. Dallas told him they needed more time. The waiter nodded and took a step back toward the kitchen, catching Dallas's attention and then nodding once more, adding a wink.

"Here's the um... brochures." The woman removed a thick envelope from her small purse. Dallas took it in his slender hand.

"Thanks." He pulled the paper from it, carefully. He felt his eyes bulge as they took in the name MORRIS MUSSEY followed by an address and a list of locations. There were several banded stacks of money in it as well. He pushed it back inside and stuffed it hastily into his jacket pocket. He took a larger than expected gulp of his wine and smiled at the woman. "I'm not usually one to get bogged down with the reasons and details of why folks want me to, well... want me. But I feel I need to in this instance."

"Simple. I'm tired of his being the albatross around the neck of my life." She smiled and it was a pointed thing, ready to maim and wound.

Dallas felt his stomach tighten. This was complicated and he hated complexity. He ran the angles in his head while he studied the woman across from him. *We kill him and then her. Both jobs are done and we already got paid. We make it look accidental and kill two birds with one stone. Nobody to point a finger or blow a whistle.*

"Are you alright, Mr. Dallas?" She laid a furtive hand on his forearm. His eyes met hers and he managed a smile—an almost goddamn sincere one. *Man, she's a looker.*

"I'm fine. Just tired. Been a long day. You want some food? I'm not hungry myself." He pulled his chair out from the table and wiped his newly damp hands on his jeans. *Get a hold of yourself, D. This is not like you, you're a cool cucumber, remember?*

He stole a glance in the direction of the only other patrons in the eatery, an old couple two tables away. "Thanks for bringing those brochures, Ma'am." He stood. Mrs. Mussey looked at him as she stood. He could see confusion in her expression and nodded. "I am sorry for leaving so abruptly."

"You should be." She paused and the tip of her tongue appeared against her painted lips and then was gone, "We might have had some fun later." She looked at him through her bangs and it was a look he knew well. She ran a hand through her hair and stood up suddenly. "But I think I'm good to go. I'll expect to hear from you when... when the trip's been booked." She flashed that smile again and this one he'd also seen before—on nature programs right before some cute critter was taken down and eaten.

"You certainly will." Dallas forgot all his chivalry and hauled his ass out the door before she even stepped away from the table.

Chapter Twelve

Skeeter's Knuckle Bucket was a ramshackle amalgamation of weathered wooden paletts, railroad ties, and repurposed barn wood planks. Other than the sign near the front entrance, there was absolutely nothing outside to indicate it was more than a pile of rubbish thrown together in a jumble of weeds.

But the inside revealed something entirely different.

For almost three decades, the Knuckle Bucket had been the best private club in the four-county region. Dice and poker games were easy enough to find. Plenty a cold drink, or stiff ones, if that was your poison. A handful of working girls rotated every few months or so, and it was up to the customer to negotiate a price if they wanted to take them upstairs for a little *ooo-la-la*. All to a soundtrack of ragged and raucous blues played lean and mean by men whittled from sorrow and sweat.

The place was run by the Kid's uncle Skeeter, who greased local palms when he had to, and used information on public figures as leverage when he needed to. Either way, the place was ignored by the law. Skeeter was in his late fifties, heavyset, bald, and with ear gauges the size of half-dollars, he looked like he stepped from the pages of a comic book.

But the main draw for the Knuckle Bucket had always been the backdoor club. The front arena was one thing—a private club but accessible to almost anyone, including a lot of the local law establishment. They might have a badge pinned to their uniform, but they weren't above throwing a hundred or two in the poker games on a weekend night or enjoying a pecker suck under the table while they watched their money fly away.

But the backdoor club was something else altogether. In this case, it was party in the front, and business in the back. It was much smaller, only made up of a short bar and several rooms, but it was a safe haven for the outcasts. Heists had been planned here, small and large. Scores. Robberies. Arsons. Worse.

It was a place where people knew when to not listen, turn their head and look the other way, and mind their own goddamn business.

Dallas and the Kid stepped to the back door and knocked. Moments later, a small panel slid open and two emerald eyes peered through the slot. "What's the pass phrase?"

Dallas took a drag from his cigarette. "I'm not saying the pass phrase."

The eyes narrowed with amusement. "Then you ain't gettin' in." The panel slid shut.

Dallas flicked his cigarette and knocked again. The panel slid open. "What's the pass phrase?"

"Henry, I've known you for about 12 years."

"Things change. Friends become enemies. Alliances crumble." The green eyes sparkled with mischief. "You get the email blast?"

Dallas gritted his teeth. "Yeah. I got the goddamn email blast."

36

"Pass phrase?"

The Kid shuffled his feet and kicked at a rock.

Dallas swallowed and exhaled slowly as he closed his eyes. "I love you. You love me. We're a happy family. With a great big-"

The panel slid shut along with the sounds of locks being undone and deep laughter as the door swung open.

Dallas stared at the gatekeeper. "Y' know, since you became a father, you turned into a real asshole."

Henry wiped at the corners of his eyes as his laughter died down. "If you have fun at your job it makes life a lot more enjoyable."

The three of them walked down a short hallway that spilled into a large room—a splintery esophagus opening into an ulcerated gut. Several round tables dotted the area, and a 12-foot bar anchored the place along the far wall.

"Gotta hit the head." The Kid mumbled and went off to the right side of the room where a small alcove painted lipstick red exposed two white doors.

Dallas took a seat at the bar and put his pack of Winstons and lighter on the scuffed pine wood bar in front of him.

The girl behind the bar stepped closer. "Hey, honey. The usual?"

Darlene was slender, her dark hair pulled back in a ponytail reaching past her shoulder blades. She had a face that was still cute, but you could tell she used to be a lot cuter—as if her beauty had been worn down over the years even though she was still in her early twenties.

Darlene gave a long pour from the bottle of Dewar's and set it in front of him with a napkin nest.

Dallas gave her a nod. "Thanks."

"So... been meaning to ask you."

"Ask me what?"

The girl leaned forward on the bar, the angles of her v-neck shirt billowing out to reveal the lines of her cleavage. "You come in from time to time and, y' know... you do your thing." Darlene reached out to touch his hand. "How come you never ask me to go upstairs for a twirl, huh? How come, Dallas? It'd be a lot of fun."

He took a sip of scotch and set the glass back down, and then Dallas patted her hand. "Well, for one, I'm not sure I have enough energy to keep up with a sexy minx like you, darlin'. You make me afraid for my health and well-being."

She smiled at his words, lighting her face up. Dallas took another sip from his drink as the Kid stepped from the men's room. She glanced at the Kid and her smile faded slightly.

"And two, it... it would be *awkward*. I can't have your brother getting all jealous and feeling inadequate because you'd be comparing he and I sexually."

"Asshole!" Darlene threw a drink coaster at him but there was still a smile on her face.

"You know I love you." Dallas chuckled and reached for his smokes.

The Kid took a seat beside him, gave a short nod to the girl. "Hey."

"Hey yourself. Ginger ale?"

"Please and thank you." His eyes were already nervous rats, darting and twitching.

Dallas wasn't completely certain of what went down between the Kid and his sister, but he knew damn well it wasn't pleasant. The Kid had come close to spilling it a few times but wasn't quite there yet. All Dallas knew for certain was that the Kid had come to live with his Uncle Skeeter and started doing the occasional job in the gray areas outside the law.

"Dallas, you shopping today?" Henry called from across the room. "I've got a private appointment in an hour that might take a while."

"Yep. Hang on." Grabbing his drink, Dallas swatted the Kid's arm. "Come on."

Henry pressed a key code on a door and the three of them stepped inside a concrete block room about twenty feet square. Three rows lined the room, with waist-high glass cases and shelving lining the walls behind them.

"What did you have in mind?" Henry reached into the first glass case and withdrew a pistol. "These are new Walther PKs. Reliable. Sturdy." He withdrew a black cylinder from the case and began screwing it onto the end of the pistol. "Silencers come standard."

Dallas shook his head.

Henry put the Walther back in the case and his face lit up with an idea. "Shotguns?"

"Too messy."

Henry moved down the aisle and Dallas stepped with him,

looking in the cases and shaking his head at each item displayed. The Kid kept close but studied items in the case as if it was a museum. He seemed fascinated. Dallas wondered whether he was soaking up the information in that big brain of his the same way he could tell you twenty fun facts about any damned musician on the planet or rattle off the color of license plates of every state like it was common knowledge.

Henry stepped away from the case toward a wall shelf. "When you absolutely, positively have to kill every—"

"Last motherfucker in the room. Yeah, I've seen the movie. But no AK-47 either. You know I'm not so big on that shit anyway."

Henry put the rifle back on the shelf, turned and leaned onto the glass case with both hands. "Dallas, what the hell are you looking for? You want plastic explosives or something? I think I can get hold of some C-4 but it'll take a week or two. Traceless poisons or something? You want to see blades?"

Dallas hadn't known what the actual plan was because it hadn't come to him yet. It was like that sometimes. Turning the job over like a puzzle in your head, this way and that. Figuring it out. But sooner or later, it always came to him.

He sipped the last of his drink, set the glass on the counter top, and then turned and smiled.

"Henry? Who do you know that deals in reptiles?"

40

CHAPTER THIRTEEN

"They shall take up serpents and if they drink any deadly thing, it shall not hurt them. They shall lay hands on the sick and they shall recover."

Dallas whispered the words and leaned his head back against his living room wall. The TV was muted and Gilligan was showing Mary Ann a pair of coconuts like it was the biggest find of the century. He grabbed the remote and turned it off.

"You okay, Dallas? Never heard you quotin' the Bible before. Never figured you knew much of it."

He turned to the Kid, then reached out a hand and clapped his leg. "I'm good. Just thinking. And yeah, I know more of it than I care to."

A flash of memory snapped in his mind, like a Polaroid developing.

Tall white tents with a podium and a jar of Strychnine glistening in the sunlight. A wire cage with a towel draped over it. Hands, so many hands. Alien sounds of the crowd. The believers. Through the flap, a swatch of sky shaped like a water moccasin's mouth.

Dallas tapped a fresh cigarette from his crumpled pack, lit it, and leaned forward on the sofa to drop the match in the ashtray. A notepad lay on the battered coffee table in front of him with some scrawled phrases—indecipherable to anyone else.

"Well, Kid. We got the who. We damn sure have that. We just need the where and when."

"Missin' the what and why, too." The Kid sat up from a lounge chair and reached for his bottle of root beer on the table. He picked it up slowly, so he could watch the condensation puddle glue the coaster to the bottom of the bottle. It was another of his games. Lift it carefully and see how high he can raise it before the coaster falls back to the table.

Dallas felt a small smile grow. If he didn't dig him so much he'd pound that kid.

Dallas shook his head. "The *what* is us ending their life. One big black exclamation point to the end of their sentence. The *why*... never count on getting a solid answer for that one. I'm sure there's more to it, but the why on this one could just be boredom."

He sucked more smoke. "I've always thought there should be some sort of justification to this line of work. An end that fits the mark, so to speak. I've always thought of myself as sort of a..." He took another drag and exhaled slowly, choosing his words. "A facilitator of proper exits."

The Kid nodded but a wash of confusion was on his face. "I'm not sure what that means."

"It means that I don't believe there's some all-knowing Sky-Daddy up in Heaven, looking down on all of us. But, I've been known to be wrong on things before. And if I am wrong and there is a God—I don't think so, but if I'm wrong—then by the time my ticket gets punched, I'll be the one with a yard-long résumé showing punishment to fit the crimes of all those I sent before me."

The coaster on the bottom of the Kid's bottle fell to the table with a soft smack and the Kid took another swallow of root beer. "This ever happen before? Both of them hiring you to take the other out?"

"I'm sure it's happened before but not to me, no. Shit like this doesn't happen by accident either. I'm not a loyal subscriber to the concept of coincidence."

"You think they're messin' with you or playing some kinda game or something?" The Kid has his nervous eyes on, darting around like goldfish after someone shook the bowl.

Dallas shook his head. "No. Nothing like that. They're on the up and up and each want the other dead. It's just that coincidences like this..." Dallas reached for his scotch and thought against it. "Nothin' Kid. Maybe this buzz is a little stronger than it should be right now. My head feels full of bees and that never amounts to anything good." He stood up from the sofa and headed down the darkened hallway. "I'm going to bed. Crash here for the night, 'cause I'm in no shape to drive you home and I don't want you walkin'. Big day tomorrow. In the morning, we'll get breakfast—lots of details to iron out."

"Can we go somewhere that has bacon and sausage?" The Kid was all eyes and smile, you'd think someone offered a poor man a bag of fifties. Dallas stopped and felt a warmth inside, fleeting but there.

"Sure, Kid. Get some sleep." He stood outside his bedroom door and listened to the Kid whisper to himself in the living room. Winding himself down to sleep. Alphabet power metal. A is for Artch.

Dallas went into his room and closed the door.

CHAPTER FOURTEEN

The Kid knew he was to be sleeping. He walked the length of the room another time. He had been through three different alphabets. He had looked at every picture—four times. Every book on the shelves. He counted the loose change on the table and stacked it. He checked the silverware drawer in the kitchen and made sure it was sorted properly. He paced some more. He talked to himself the entire time. He sat on the edge of the sofa and picked up the remote for the television. He clicked it on and muted it right away. Gomer Pyle was making his dumb old donkey faces and the Kid changed the channel. News. More news. *Mama's Family.* More news. *Three's Company.* More news.

"Ooh." He stopped on an infomercial about a new model vacuum cleaner. The Kid sat, leaned forward, and turned the volume up just enough to be barely audible. He didn't really need it. He'd watched this one at home enough to have it memorized. "It's the Ordin Dustsucker Prism Model number 3409-T. It has a canister system." He started bouncing his leg. "It's available in a deluxe and a..."

"Kid! TV off and eyes closed, dammit!" Dallas hollered from back the hall.

"Okay. Sorry." The Kid winced as he turned off the set. He took off his sneakers and leaned back on the sofa cushions. He felt the softness of the pillow under his head. He lay there and stared at the now-dead screen. The teeny tiny dot in the middle was fading. "That Ordin is a great vacuum cleaner." He whispered it a few more times before he finally nodded off.

CHAPTER FIFTEEN

"It's all about routines. We're creatures of habit. Some might be a short habit, others a lifetime's worth, but those habits make people predictable."

The Kid nodded and dipped a crisp slice of bacon into a puddle of syrup on his plate. He took a bite and chewed slowly, savoring it. A single sausage link remained on his plate like a patient soldier.

Dallas drank from his cup of black coffee. "Once you see the routines, you can use them to your advantage. More we know, the easier it should be. Easier to follow a path than make one."

The waitress stepped to the table and the Kid glanced up. She was a pretty girl, barely in her twenties. She smiled at him and his eyes flitted back to his bacon. Eye contact was not a capability of the Kid.

She turned to Dallas and held up a coffee pot. "You fellas want some more go-juice?"

Dallas smiled back at her. "I think I'm juiced up enough this morning. Just the check, darlin'."

She pulled a tablet from her apron and peeled off a check with a practiced one-handed move, leading Dallas, for a fleeting moment, to wonder what other ways she could use her nimble hands. He shook it away and reached for his wallet as she walked away.

"So now what?" The Kid stuffed the sausage into his mouth. He wiped his mouth with a paper napkin and folded it in half and half again, tucking it beneath his plate.

Peeling a ten-dollar bill and a slip of paper from his billfold, Dallas put the cash on the receipt and his coffee mug on top of it. He slid a slip of paper across the table toward the Kid and lowered his voice.

"Now, we observe. Morris Mussey works as an investment consultant at this address. The Mrs... well, we're going to have to do a little homework on her. No job and a lot of idle time on her hands during the day." Dallas eased out of the booth. "Those two things combined and the way she looks..." He glanced at the Kid, shook his head and made a low whistle. "She's putting some time in on her back somewhere."

"Wha... ohhhh." The light bulb went off in the Kid's mind.

"But this job is unusual." Dallas turned and nodded at the waitress behind the counter. "Afternoon, darlin'. Thank you."

The girl raised one of those slender hands and waved to accent her smile. The Kid lowered his head and gave a lackluster wave back.

"We need to get them together." The door jingled as the Kid pulled it open." And how do we get two people who hate each other enough to snuff the other out, together in the same place at the same time?"

The Kid opened his mouth to offer an idea but hesitated. Dallas held up a finger and stopped walking.

His jeans pocket vibrated again and Dallas pulled a beaten up

48

flip phone from it and answered. "Yep."

Henry's voice was on the other end. "That fix-it shop you were asking me about? I found one for you. Has a place out on Grange Road, 'bout a mile or so past the junkyard. Can't miss it. Sky blue double-wide on the left."

"Thanks for coming through, pal. I knew you would." Dallas stuffed the phone back in his pocket. "One more piece lined up in the puzzle. Now to see how our benefactors spend their days."

CHAPTER SIXTEEN

"Looks like the sky at the beginning of *Search For Tomorrow*." The Kid spoke as they pulled over to the side of the road, across from the building.

Dallas kept his hand on the keys and looked at the boy. "What?" The smoke from the cigarette in the corner of his mouth flooded his right eye even and he winked it nearly closed.

"*Search For Tomorrow* was a soap opera that ran on CBS from 1951 until 1986. It originally ran fifteen-minute episodes for the first seven years before going to half-hour episode length."

The boy paused to swallow a breath and Dallas stared at him. He wasn't actually mad or even annoyed, just kind of stunned as these outbursts usually left him.

"It was produced by Proctor and Gamble. That's why they call them soap operas because most of the backers and producers of these early drama programs were soap and cleaning product manufacturers."

The Kid was wired tight today. His leg was going a mile a minute and he was doing the hand thing. *Not Good.* Dallas looked at the trailer and back at his passenger. He pinched the cigarette from his lips and flicked it out the window. The smoke he blew out blended with the misting rain.

"Kid. You wait here. Don't touch anything. I'll be right back."

"But Dallas—"

"Don't. Just don't. You stay here and anchor yourself. Alphabet Funk. Control and calm. You read me?"

Heavy sigh, like a bag of heavy cement, but the Kid nodded.

"Like a fucking book." He pounded his fist on the dashboard like a spoiled brat.

Dallas closed his door in the middle of "C is for Captain Sky." He walked briskly in the light rain. The trailer was listing to one side, more noticeable once he was on the small porch that jutted from the roadside—a sneering tongue from a taunter. He stole a glance back to the car and saw the Kid sitting there, mouth moving and hands dancing. He almost smiled until the sadness he often felt when it came to that boy flooded in and snuffed out the flame of it. He raised a hand to knock when the door opened inward and a gruff voice invited him to enter.

"Henry never said who it was!" Dallas beamed as he took several giant steps to eat the distance between the door and the sofa. "My God, Benny, how long has it been?" He leaned and threw an arm around the old man. The man was as ancient as dirt and just as dark and dusty.

"Fuckin' Henry never told me it was you neither, Dally!" Moist laughter followed.

"Been a lot of years. More 'an I can count. Then again, I never made it past the fifth grade."

The old man laughed—a brittle breeze over crooked tombstone

teeth. Dallas stole a quick glance at the two young black men who stood in the kitchen. One had a pistol in his belt and the other was rolling a joint. They looked unamused, but Dallas didn't much care. He sat down on the chair next to the end of the couch where the old man rested. He gently patted the geezer's arm.

"He's harmless." Dallas spoke when he saw the kitchen boys craning to peer out the window at what he assumed was the Kid talking to himself in the car.

"Who he talkin' to?" Gun Belt asked.

"Himself. He's fine. Ignore him." Dallas re-affixed his smile and turned to the old man.

"So Henry said you could help me? I have a... less than normal request." He smiled bigger allowing all of his straight and slightly yellowed teeth an audience.

"He filled me in." The old man fidgeted with the oxygen tube around his neck. Dallas helped him arrange it so the plugs were in his nostrils. The old man smiled and breathed a few deep nose breaths. "Used to think that ol' Samson Gallows was the oddest duck I ever met. 'Specially after he bought that fuckin' mummy's head." Benny laughed a little. "But this... the fuck you up to, Dally?" He grinned. Gun Belt stepped away from the window and had his hand down his pants fiddling with whatever lived in that dank darkness.

"You two." Benny barked. Gun Belt and Joint Roller stopped and looked at him, saucer-eyed.

"Git gone. My boy, D and I have some talkin' to do and we don't need no chaperones."

"But Gramps."

"You Gramps me one more time they gonna be pulling this air tube out your dickhole. That is if you can keep your fuckin' greasy-ass hands off it long enough for me to gain access. I never seen a fucker so inclined to touch hisself as you. Like a fuckin' monkey in the zoo. Go on. Get outta here. Go down the store and buy me some strawberry sherbet. Take about fifteen minutes. Shit, take a lot longer. I'm sick of the sight of y'all."

Benny fastened his directive with a hard stare and Dallas smiled. Benny was still a scary fucker. The two men left, loudly, and walked around to the back of the trailer, pulling out a few minutes later in a Dodge older than they were but with expensive rims on the tires. Ridiculous. Dallas sat there a moment and listened to the old man breathe. He smiled at his old friend, one of his earliest mentors. "Why did they take that shitty truck with the stupid rims when you have that nice new Escalade around the side?"

"'Coz I don't want them stinkin' up my ride with they reefer and pussy shenanigans." Benny chuckled and then his mouth went serious before he continued.

"So... Dallas, really? Fucking rattlers?"

The smile Dallas donned at that moment would have outdone the Cheshire Cat.

CHAPTER SEVENTEEN

Dallas hit a bump in the road and even through the back seat, the sound of the rattles were loud. The Kid glanced to the back and then to Dallas. "Snakes are ooky. I don't wanna have to touch 'em. He give you snake grabber things? I'm not touching them."

"Mmhmm. In the back seat along with four shots of antivenin if we should need it."

He could feel the Kid staring at him. That damned leg going a mile a minute.

"I hope to hell we don't need it."

"Same here." Dallas grinned wider and the sounds of the rattling grew louder. You could almost hear the hatred seasoning the noise. There was a part of him that wondered if he should have asked Benny to silence them and cut the rattles off, but he knew better. In the end, it would be fitting. Maybe even poetic.

The rattlesnake was wrapped around the pastor's arm and woven through his fingers as the sermon about damnation and salvation rolled on. Pastor held it over his head and Dallas could see its tongue flicker in and out, tasting the air. Its eyes hard chips of polished stone, watching all, like a small omnipotent god. It had seen Dallas all right, and Dallas had seen it back, as he listened to the sermon about the serpent and God.

The pastor preached on and the congregation stood and sat, stood and sat. Later, Dallas knew there would be music and some dancing and sometimes people would start speaking the languages of Heaven itself. Dallas often wondered what the people were saying with their odd noises and sounds. He didn't understand it and it scared him a little.

He preached with the rattlesnake on his hand and arm and the serpent moved and bobbed along with his motions. Snake in one hand, Bible in the other—the pastor raised them both overhead.

The jars of Strychnine were brought out onto the pulpit, and the snake was put back into its container. It had kept staring at Dallas, gently weaving its head side to side like a rusted weathervane in a soft breeze. A Pastor's assistant had pulled a white cloth over the tank but through the rest of the sermon, Dallas could feel its gaze still focused on him.

The soft skin of Mama's hand sliding against his palm and her smile— genuine but somehow insincere at the same time. Feeling her warmth as he leaned against her shoulder and whispered in her ear. "Will I have friends there, Mama?"

"Dallas!" The Kid had his hands out against the dash as Dallas instinctively slammed the brakes, making the car skid to a stop on the gravel road. Pebbles *thunked* under them. The tank thumped against the rear trunk well, igniting the fury of the rattlers again. Dust blew past them on both sides.

Grange Road had come to an end. Dallas gave the Kid a sheepish glance. "Sorry Kid. Must've been daydreaming a little there. The Kid was all eyes and he'd gone paler than usual.

"I might have to burn these underpants." The Kid said slowly, smiling slightly.

"Young man, I've taken you to the laundromat, you oughta burn them *all*."

He turned left and reached for his Winstons. Time to drop off the cargo and find the routines of the Musseys. Lots of daylight left and he didn't want to burn it.

CHAPTER EIGHTEEN

"Dallas?"

"Huh?" There was a very small crinkling sound as he sucked smoke through the burning tobacco of his cigarette. The sound would not have registered to anyone but the Kid.

"Think I could crash at your house again?"

Dallas held the smoke in his mouth, an amorphous prisoner. He gazed at the Kid sidelong and tried not to grin. Fucked if he wasn't a softie for this boy. He really felt for him. He understood what it was like to be alone, growing up alone. He wore his loneliness like a tattoo snaking around his torso and waist, an anchor he could never shake. He parted his lips a little and let the cancer ghost free. He knew the doctors and teachers put the Kid on the *spectrum* wherever the fuck that was. But all he knew was this kid was as honest as the morning dew. Had no concept of pretense or manipulative fuckery, not in any malicious sense. He couldn't lie his way out of a paper bag. He was untainted by social convention and what you asked for, you got, no frills or bullshit. Pure honesty. The street value on that shit alone was incredible.

"We'll see, Kid."

The Kid smiled and turned to look out the window. It was that odd part of the day, when day was approaching a stage of dying and fading into night. It was a growing bruise. He put his hand against the window and stared at the trailer. Its unlit windows were blackened eyes. He always thought of black eyes when he looked at this shitbox. The plastic that Darrell had taped over the windows years ago beckoned like spectral fingers. Like that ghost's hand at the beginning of Scooby-Doo cartoons. The Kid sighed and smiled. He reached for the door handle and felt Dallas put a hand on his shoulder.

"Stay put."

The Kid turned and looked at the older man as he got out of the car. He walked around to the trunk and opened it up. The Kid watched him walk up the rotting steps of the trailer and kick the door—once. It opened like a drunkard's mouth. Dallas disappeared inside with something red cradled in his arms. The Kid grew tense. His fingers worried at the vinyl of the armrest. His leg was skipping beats.

CHAPTER NINETEEN

The trailer was worse inside than out. You'd not think that possible. The stench that greeted Dallas confirmed a dark suspicion he had been holding for well on a few months now. He unscrewed the lid of the gas can and started sloshing the liquid around the kitchen. Mice screeched as they fled the giant in their midst. Dallas took out his penlight and focused the beam around the room. Cereal boxes and mac and cheese containers filled the corner, obscuring the window so no light touched the mess. He saw the mice were cohabitating with roaches and apparently living in harmony. Humans could learn a thing or two. A dead cat lay by the doorway and had been stripped nearly to the bones—a mouse chewed at the dried hide of the cat's back paw. Fucking creepily ironic. Dallas backed out, pouring as he went.

He held the penlight between his teeth and steadied the emptying canister as he splashed gas in the corners. Dallas only needed points to ignite and the rest of this shithole would just give up the ghost. He turned to side step the broken coffee table and stopped.

The penlight nearly fell from his mouth so he had to will it not to gape. He was next to the couch and upon it was what must have been the Kid's mama.

"Christ." The corpse was wet. *Moist* was probably a more accurate term, but he disliked that word. Her rotted flesh had sort of slid from the bones and laid around the lower areas of her body in congealed clumps swarming with movement. White things. Buzzing things. Dallas saw a swatch of floral print that wasn't mired in putrescence and mold. He turned his head and slopped some petrol over her.

"Kid..." Dallas spoke into the silent room, his voice shaking, and he felt tears threatening to leak from his eyes. He put the blame on the fumes but Dallas knew better. He stomped back down the hall and into the bedroom. He found Darrel in there—his state of decomposition no worse than that of the Kid's mother, but Dallas noted the man's head was not entirely there.

He sneered at the man and remembered the few stories the Kid had told him about this lovely sumbitch. He kicked something and looked down at the hammer lying by the bed. Dallas emptied the can and sat it beside the corpse, then picked up three of the *Hustler* magazines from the bedside table and rolled one up as he made his way back through the doorway. He lit the end with his lighter, and when it took, he dropped it to the floor. There was a *whoosh* as the flames began to devour the rotting carpet and lick the walls, beating a path to the bed and the dead bastard rotting in it. Dallas kept walking. He was openly crying now, just thinking of that poor boy doing time in this place. "Burning the bridge behind us, Kid."

He repeated the act in the living room and kitchen and then stepped out onto the small wooden pallet that served as a porch. He stood and waited until the heat began to pummel his back. His hair sticking to his neck. Dallas looked across the road at the car and the Kid gawping out the window, smiling like it was Christmas and crying at the same time. He stuck his fists in his pockets and crossed to the car.

"Why'd you do that, Dallas?"

"I came to cast fire on the earth, and would that it were already kindled." Dallas pulled a cigarette from the pack and lit it with a flick of his Zippo.

"For someone who don't believe in God, you sure know a lot of the Bible."

"I know. Weird ain't it?" They watched as metal expanded and flames pushed through the roof in a plot to touch the sky.

"Goodbye, Mama." The Kid whispered and Dallas kept his gaze out the window so his tears would not be witnessed. He managed a slight smile when the Kid followed it with "Fuck You, Darrell."

Dallas hunched forward and put the car in gear. As it started to roll he spoke. "Let's go home, Kid."

CHAPTER TWENTY

Morris pulled the banded stacks of bills from the wall safe and set them on his desk. It would be best to put this somewhere else for safekeeping until loose ends were tied up, in case anything went wrong. He ignored the stock and bond certificates and documents in the safe and turned to his desk, appraising the money before him.

Cash is king. It was just about one of the only things his father had taught him, but it was an important lesson. Slowly and quietly, he had been accumulating his nest egg. A grand here, five thousand there—it had taken time, but he was staring at close to four hundred grand on his desk. His accountant knew where to push this and pull that to keep it off the books and far away from Victoria's long nose. That bitch had a sniffer for money all right—like a bloodhound on the trail of a lost kid. But not this time.

He stood and stepped to his office windows, using a finger to part the blinds and look outside. He had been feeling something was off lately, and it was making him twitchy. Maybe it was only that things were coming to an end. Excitement maybe? Morris didn't know, but the last time he had felt this way, he had learned Victoria had hired someone to follow him around town. Nosy bitch. He scanned the cars parked within sight on the street. Nothing out of the ordinary. He was getting paranoid.

Soon. What had the man said? Seven days? Ten at the most?

Morris stuffed the reams of cash into a cardboard box and taped the lid shut. He grabbed a marker from his desk and printed in all caps across the top: RECIEPTS. Fuck, this was one of the *I-before-E-except-words.* Screw it—he had no time for that nonsense.

Beside the box, Morris glanced at a full-color brochure with a shitty too-excited font across the top: *EXPERIENCE COSTA RICA!* He smiled to himself. Oh yes. Yes, he *would* experience it—that and so much more, as soon as the fucking chain was taken from around his neck.

CHAPTER TWENTY ONE

The cucumbers felt so deliciously cool against her eyes that Victoria released a long sigh and felt her shoulders relax. She could feel the volcanic mud mask working on the pores of her face. The soothing music of the spa—Enya or Kitaro or some Yanni shit—was tacky and expected, but she let her mind drift.

Once Morris was... dispatched... what then? She figured the insurance would hold her over very well while she put the business up for sale. Then the summerhouse in the Outer Banks. Getting everything in order to live the rest of her delectable life.

But then what?

The idea had occurred to Victoria that she would no longer be tethered to this region without Morris around. She could literally go *anywhere* she felt like.

And Chad? What about him? Victoria sighed again and adjusted the towel wrapped beneath her armpits. *Maybe I'll get him a nice parting gift, but that's about it. That ball of yarn is to be discarded as well.*

Where did Casablanca take place? Was that in Spain? Morocco? One of the places where men sweated through their linen suits.

Morocco. Yeah, that would be a good start. A little trip to Morocco to let all of life's weight slough off. Some time on the beach and maybe a tryst with a handsome high roller on vacation.

The thought of wild sex with a tanned stranger in a beach resort made Victoria wriggle in place and she widened her legs slightly.

How hot would that be? One of those wide tropical ceiling fans overhead. The sound of crashing waves outside. Drinks with paper umbrellas in them. And a muscled naked man with tan lines, glistening with sex sweat.

Victoria smiled and cracked her mud mask. *That was okay. There's time for a lot of decadence in the future.* She let her fingers do the walking and didn't give a shit if anyone walked in.

Chapter Twenty Two

"Hey kid? Habla inglés?" Dallas pulled his old aviator sunglasses down and peered over the top of them at a young dark-skinned kid wearing a red Jordan basketball jersey and baggy jean shorts. He appeared about eight or nine years old at most. He didn't get off the seat of his bike, but walked it over closer to the car.

"Yeah, I speak English. 'Sup?" His eyes were untrusting, hands on the grips of the bike and one foot resting on a pedal, ready to haul ass if things got weird.

Good, Dallas thought. That means he's cautious. "You want to make an easy twenty bucks?"

The boy scrunched his face up, looking at Dallas like he was an old pervert cruising the neighborhood. "I ain't gettin' in that mothafuckin' car with you two." He stepped the bike back a little. His face grew darker, his brows forming a V over his eyes. "I ain't no faggot neither, so get that shit out of your minds."

Dallas turned to the Kid. "You hear the mouth on him? *Jeeeezus.*" He took his sunglasses off and used them to emphasize his words to the boy. "First of all, *faggot* is not an acceptable word when you're talking to me. Or anyone really. You like being called a wetback or beaner or a spic?"

"Fuck no, I don't!"

66

"Then there you go. So let's erase that word, and hell, all of them from your memory. Don't use 'em. To me or anyone. You're better than that."

"What the fuck you want?" For a kid, this one had less patience than most.

"I'm not asking you to get in the car." Dallas put his sunglasses back on and pulled a twenty-dollar bill out from his pocket. He held it so the boy could see it, and then tore it in half right down the middle. "Half now. Half when you're done." He flicked one half out and it floated down to the sidewalk in little circular spins like a wounded bird.

The boy eased forward and picked up the torn half, stuffing it in his pocket. "What y'all want me to do? And 'member I ain't suckin' no dicks!"

Dallas held up a small black box in his hand, showing it to the boy, then he pointed down the street ahead of them. "You see that silver Lexus up there, 'bout ten cars up?"

The boy looked away and then back. He nodded.

"This thing's got a magnet. Go put it on the rear passenger side of the car, underneath the fender where the wheel is. You got it? Nod if you understand?" Dallas waited for the boy to nod, then he held it out to him. It was snatched away quickly—still cautious—and the boy rode off up the street. Dallas watched him go up the street and past the Lexus.

"He's not gonna do it." The Kid was slumped in his seat a little, watching the boy.

"He'll do it. He's just taking inventory of the area."

The boy scanned the area and then circled back their direction. When he got close to the Lexus, he paused, set his bike down and bent to one knee, as if he was tying his sneaker, then popped back onto his bike and rode toward them.

Dallas held out the other half of the torn bill and the boy didn't even slow down as he rode by and plucked the rest of the twenty without a word and continued down the street. As Dallas watched him in the side mirror, the bastard flipped him the bird. Dallas smiled and shook his head.

"Well, now we can have eyes on both of them at the same time." Dallas reached into a backpack in the rear seat and pulled out a digital tablet. He touched a few spots on screen and handed it to the Kid. "Take a look at this thing."

"I've never messed with one of these, Dallas."

"Makes two of us, then." Dallas leaned over and pointed. "See that blinking dot there on the map? That's the car."

"When did you even get this?" The Kid held the tablet as if it was going to break in his hands, but he touched the screen to see what it could do.

"Benny doesn't only sell reptiles. I got a package deal from him. Besides..." Dallas pulled the car away from the curb. "We needed to follow both of their routines at the same time. Work smarter, not harder and all that shit."

The Kid was keeping an eye on the green dot as Dallas kept driving down the street. "This is cool."

68

"Better than Donkey Kong?"

The Kid raised his head and gave Dallas a smirk. "Now you're just talking crazy. I was always a Pac Man guy myself, unless there was a Dig Dug machine around."

Damn boy had his quirks, but he was a good kid. Dallas returned the smirk. "Now that we've got the Missus taken care of, it's time to go check on the man of the house."

CHAPTER TWENTY THREE

"So you think he's got some side muff or what?" The Kid tore off a piece of beef jerky and chewed.

Dallas lifted a small box and shook a dime-sized white tablet into his palm. He popped it into his mouth and chewed. "Did you just say muff?"

"Yeah." The Kid smiled. "Would you prefer moose knuckle or whisker biscuit? Maybe minge or bush?"

Dallas chewed hard and willed himself not to smile as he continued. "Well, a man like him, with power and money?" He turned to look at the Kid. "Wouldn't be surprised if that's part of the reason for the hit. A hot piece of ass will make a man do crazy things."

"Furburger is what got us kicked out of Eden." The Kid tacked on with no trace of a smile.

"Furburger?" Dallas couldn't hide his smirk anymore. "That's it. I'm hiding all my Playboys from you."

They were parked behind a silver minivan blocking them from the office building Morris owned. It gave a thin slice for line of sight to the structure, but it was more than enough. Morris had arrived promptly at 7:00 that morning, well ahead of the employees. It was now nearing 10:00 AM and they hadn't seen him since.

"What was your first time like?"

"I was in tenth grade and it was with a little brunette girl named Yvette who had her—"

"No, no. Not that." The Kid had a sideways grin on his face. He peeled plastic away from the rest of his beef jerky. "The first person you killed. Your first hit."

"First person I killed and my first hit are two very different things." Dallas kept staring at the office building, then rolled his window down, spit and shook his head. "This nicotine gum tastes like cat ass in a hot garbage bag." He reached into his jacket pocket and withdrew a pack of Winstons. "I'll tell you about my first hit."

He lit a cigarette and stared at the building. "I was 19 years old and there was this guy in the neighborhood, everyone called him Dave the Cage, or just Cage for short. He was a bookie, ran numbers on horses and football and shit. Had a house up in Dalton Hills, was doing damn well for himself, but he went deep with the wrong fuckin' people."

Dallas took a drink of cold coffee from a foam cup in the center console. "I'd been collecting for Cage for oh... about a year at that point. He was all right to me. Not great. Not bad. I'd go visit these coked-out deadbeats who placed a bad bet with a fuckin' spread that..." Dallas moved his hands apart as he glanced at the Kid. "No goddamn way the football game was gonna end that way, y'know? These way out there bets no one in their right fuckin' mind would lay money on. I'd go collect the cash. Had to break some shit here and there, but whatever, that was the job. I was good at it."

"I'll bet you were." The Kid tore off another piece of jerky.

"What I didn't know is that Cage had been taking his profits and betting on the same sort of lunatic shit with the *Chernyy Kulak*, this Russian outfit that called themselves the Black Fist. Mean sons o' bitches. Sooner cut your fuckin' balls off than wait to collect."

A white van pulled up to the office building and Dallas watched as a man in a tan uniform stepped free with a large cardboard box and walk inside. The man came out moments later and pulled out of the lot.

"I was coming out of this guy's apartment one night, a loser named Antoine who was continually pushing the limits of paying his debts to Cage. He got off with a broken nose that night but handed over the two grand he owed. I'm getting ready to get in my car and this giant fuckin' Russkie approaches me. Just what you'd expect— baldheaded with fists the size of canned hams and no neck. Built like a goddamn T-rex." Dallas took a long drag from his cigarette and let the smoke drift from his mouth as he continued. "One thing led to another and next thing I know, I'm getting paid twenty large to put Cage underground."

"Your boss?"

"I mean... yeah, I guess you could say that. He wasn't really my boss, but sure."

"He was the guy that paid you to do stuff for him. That's a boss."

"Technically, yeah, but well... there was no respect involved so it's kind of different."

The Kid pulled a bottle of root beer from the console and sipped it. "How'd you do it?"

"Cage had a habit of hitting the local speakeasy at the end of his day, which, was really more like morning because he was taking bets all goddamn night. He'd have a pint or two some nights. Other days, if he had lost his ass, he'd get shitcanned off of gin. At the time, with being in so deep with the Russians, Cage was getting smashed almost every damn night." Dallas took another drink of coffee and made a face.

"I waited in his driveway for him one night. Cage didn't get home till almost four in the morning and was piss drunk, stumbling out of his fuckin' car. He made his way to the front and I jumped him, spun him around and tripped him up and he fell. Wasn't how I planned it, but Cage slammed his head and neck on the brick steps to his front porch. Big guy or not, it sounded like someone breaking a stalk of celery when he landed." He took a drag off his Winston and though Dallas was watching the building, he was also staring at the memory.

"I left the door to his car open and walked. Next day I got the *attaboy job well done* from the Black Fist. I did more than a few jobs for them over the next decade or so."

The Kid crumpled up the plastic wrapper from the jerky and stuffed it in his jacket pocket. "You ever... ever feel bad about it?"

"About taking down the Cage? Hell no. If I hadn't done it, someone else would have. He was into the Russians for almost a quarter mil and doing his damnedest to make that hole even deeper. I did him a favor compared to what would have happened if the

Russians had taken it into their own hands."

"Yeah?"

Dallas took the last drag and flicked the cigarette out the window. "Fuck yeah. Give those guys handcuffs, a chair and a rope and they'll make you confess to anything. And don't get me started about their fuckin' watermelon diets."

"What the hell is that?"

"Nothin' Kid. Point is, no, snuffing out the Cage didn't ever make me feel bad."

A flicker of movement at the office building and Dallas narrowed his focus. Morris stepped from the building, heading toward his car. He was carrying a briefcase in one hand and a backpack slung over his shoulder.

Dallas grunted and the Kid questioned. "What's up?"

"I've got a feeling... that Mr. Mussey is breaking his daily routine."

CHAPTER TWENTY FOUR

The Kid sulked on the couch at the house. Dallas had deemed him too wound up to safely take along as he trailed Mussey. The Kid sat nearest the chair, staring into nothing and making the pictures on the end table tremble with his leg shaking.

"I'm not too wound up." He took a deep breath and then another. "I'm an excitable boy." He smiled. "I dug up her grave and built a cage from her bones." He laughed and it was more than a little manic.

The Kid stood and headed to the kitchen as the phone rang. He looked at it. It rang again. He wasn't allowed to answer it but he couldn't stand the noise. It was a million times louder for him than a normal person. The Kid grabbed the receiver in mid-ring. "Hello?"

"Dallas?"

"Um... yes." The Kid's eyes were trying to dart right out of his head.

"I want to hire you to do a job. Is that how this goes? I need someone gone."

"Yes. Okay," the Kid answered.

"I want to kill the husband of the woman I'm fucking. What's that gonna run?"

"That's $10,000." The Kid fired off the first big number that popped into the jumbled mess of his head.

"Okay. I'll get it to you along with a picture and an address. That all you need?"

"That's it. Bring that stuff to thirty-four Blochwood Lane. Across the road from where the trailer burned down. I'll meet you there tomorrow night at eleven. What's your name?" The Kid was struggling to recall any phone etiquette he knew. The sound of his own voice in his ears was jangling his nerves.

"Chad."

"Okay, Chad." With that the Kid hung up the phone and sat down on the couch. He smiled. "I'll show Dallas. I'll take Chad's money myself and take care of the hubby." He started to shake his leg again.

Chapter Twenty Five

Officer Wesley had been waiting for this break for nearly two years. It had taken that long to get this close to his target and for the last two months he'd been sitting in this cramped up van, stinking of old coffee, old farts, and his own body odor, listening in on phone calls—hoping for something concrete to nail the man called Dallas for his "job."

Now he had enough concrete to lay a foundation. After weeks and months of nothing but random, once-in-a-while calls that amounted to gibberish—TV shows and vacations, which were no doubt coded but no one could do anything with it.

But tonight, the fucker had finally slipped up. Wesley tilted his head sharply to the left and the bones cracked like walnuts. He took off his sweaty headphones and climbed up to the driver's seat. He felt like a man who'd been under an X-ray apron for weeks that had finally had it lifted from him. He started the engine and slowly drove off down the street. As Wesley turned at the corner, he paid no mind to the older man with the winking cigarette driving slowly in the opposite direction. Curtis Mayfield wafted from the open window.

CHAPTER TWENTY SIX

Dallas had followed Mr. Mussey out of town until the man cut a hard right-turn on the gravel driveway to Brenner's Junkyard. The place used to be a good source for car parts but had been abandoned for the last ten years since the old man had died with no kids to take over the place. Now it was massive piles of rusted vehicles surrounded by thickly wooded hillside, a place for the local teens to play stinky-finger with the town sluts and get stoned out of the eyes of the law.

Mussey drove between the stacks of vehicles while Dallas pulled off into another row and killed the car's engine. Dallas needed to avoid being seen, and he was glad he had dropped the Kid off at home earlier. Truth was, Dallas hadn't had much of a choice—the Kid had been amped the fuck up since Dallas had given him the GPS tracking pad. Excitement maybe? The Kid's damn leg had been twitching hard enough to make the loose change in his pockets rattle. It was like he was jonesing for coke or something, but Dallas knew better—the Kid rarely even drank a beer. Drugs were out of the question.

When Dallas had dropped him off, the Kid was a scolded puppy, with sad, hurt eyes and a touch of anger. He had let the Kid in the house and told him to do the ABCs on pre-70s country.

Dallas left the car behind and crept around the second row of the junkyard. Pintos and old station wagons stacked in columns. Explorers crumpled like wadded paper. Here and there, an antique Chevy with one remaining headlight, appearing like a one-eyed pundit ready to tell tales of its youth. He kept moving ahead, hunched over until he heard the engine of Mussey's car stop running. A car door opened and closed. Dallas knelt down behind the rusted out shell of an old Ford pickup. His knees began to blaze with the reminder he was no spring chicken and that the return to standing from a hunkered position would not be as easy as it had been in his youth.

Mussey slung a backpack over his shoulder and paused at the rear of his car, looking around. Satisfied, he approached the side of a midnight blue Ford Escape, and stopped to look around the junkyard again. This fucker was as paranoid as a coked-up conspiracy theorist. Mussey eased open the rear door and stuffed the backpack inside. He stepped back and appeared to study his work, then brushed his hands off and returned to his car.

Dallas waited and watched. The man drove out of the junkyard with a cloud of gravel dust in his wake. He stood and went to the crumpled Escape, and then opened the door and pulled the backpack free of its hiding spot.

The noise of the zipper sounded louder than it should against the backdrop of cicadas. It made Dallas feel uneasy and exposed. But when he peeled back the canvas to reveal the contents, the uneasy feeling broke apart and gave way to a wide grin on his face. Banded stacks of motivation. A lot of it.

He zipped the backpack closed again and walked a single car to the left—a metallic pink Geo Tracker with a busted windshield and no hood. Dallas opened the driver's side door and stuffed the backpack tight beneath the seat. There was a stiff, moldy sweatshirt lying on the passenger seat and he pulled it down over the bag for camouflage.

Wiping his hands on his thighs as he stood, Dallas smiled as he made his way back to his car.

CHAPTER TWENTY SEVEN

"The number's tied to a local handyman and small project construction guy. One-man show it looks like. Name is Chad Rollins."

Wesley checked his watch. "Okay. Call me back in two hours. No, I'll call you back in two hours."

"What all do you want?" The voice on the phone sounded very tired.

Wesley leaned back against his couch. "Everything. Blood type, religion. Who his first and latest girlfriend is. His favorite fucking color. I want to know if the motherfucker's circumcised or not. If Mexican food makes him fart, I wanna know what they smell like... everything and anything."

"Done." That poor little four-letter word nearly smothered under the sigh delivering it.

Wesley ended the call, reached for the foam cup of tequila, and took a swallow. He looked at his living room and the three unopened cardboard boxes against the bare wall. They were the only things in the room besides the couch he sat on, an antique coffee table from his dear dead grandmother, and the picture of him and Sarah in a cheap ass frame that stood on it. Sarah. He wanted to smile when he thought of her, but couldn't get the expression up and working. They had really been planning on making a life together, before...

He raised the foam cup toward the photo and took another drink. "Cheers to you, babe. It was a good run, and I don't blame you for leaving, but we can't change what we are."

The burn of the alcohol felt good as it reached his stomach. He raised his hand and stared at his wedding ring, then poured a splash of tequila on his ring finger. Wesley dropped the now empty cup on the floor and started singing "*I've Always Been Crazy"* in what was probably the worst Waylon impression ever, and twisted the ring free. He studied the wet gold for a moment.

"No." He slung the ring against the wall and it bounced off, rolling to a far corner of the room and fell still. He leaned his head back against the wall behind the couch and closed his eyes. The sad-edged smile he'd forced warped into a sneer.

"No, we can't change what the fuck we are."

Chapter Twenty Eight

The smell of macaroni and slightly burnt hot dogs greeted Dallas as he walked into his house.

The Kid was standing at the kitchen counter, scooping some noodles onto a plate. He turned to Dallas, smiling. "Here."

That warm flutter rose inside his chest again and Dallas couldn't help but smile, regardless of how the Kid had been acting earlier in the day. "Well, holy shit. Good job, Chef Boyardee." He pulled a beer from the six-pack of Budweiser he held and handed the remaining five to the Kid. Dallas took the plate and made his way to his chair in the living room. "Put those in the fridge, please." The Kid did as he was asked and followed the older man into the living room, a hyperactive shadow.

"How'd it go?" The Kid had his ever-present root beer in his hand. His expression was excited but calm at the same time. Expectant maybe? He had asked the question, and then turned his eyes downward.

Dallas had been a student of body language for most of his life. It was the little things, really. By now, it had gone past a habit and was just a part of how he was. How he existed. Survived.

"Everything go okay while I was gone?" He scooped a forkful of pasta into his mouth, never steered his eyes from the Kid's face.

The Kid glanced at him and back to his root beer. "Yeah, yeah. I just hung out. Made dinner. All was good."

"You remember to feed the snakes?"

"I remembered but didn't do it. I'm scared of 'em, Dallas. That rattling makes my teeth itch."

"There's nothing to fear if you move slow and calm. I'll take care of it before I turn in for the night. Don't worry on it." Dallas took a swig of his beer and looked at the plate of pasta and processed meat on the arm of the chair.

"Want me to get you some ketchup?" The Kid stood and gestured to the kitchen. Dallas nodded and forked a chunk of pink meat into his mouth. The smile he followed it with was a fake a car salesman's promise.

Dallas glanced around the room. His mail was stacked up on the coffee table, the magazines all alternating so the pile remained even and straight. A quick look at the handful of DVDs on a small bookshelf and he noticed they were arranged alphabetically. There wasn't a film of dust on top of the TV anymore. The rugs were aligned and their fringes all smoothed out.

Well shit. Part of him felt bad that whatever was fucking with the Kid inside made him act this way. Dallas wasn't sure that would ever go away. For now, it was part of who and what the Kid was. But maybe he could learn to harness it like a super power.

Over time, maybe.

"It went well. Learned some useful things. The puzzle is coming together." Dallas stabbed a slice of hot dog and shoveled it in his mouth. He was not a fan of them, kept them solely for the Kid, but he was for damn certain not about to hurt the boy's feelings. He made a show of smiling while he masticated the lips and assholes of various farm animals. It took his patented steely reserve to swallow them down.

"Good. Good." The Kid chewed his bottom lip, then set his root beer down and went to a tall bookshelf in the corner of the room. He reached to the top and pulled down a wooden case. "Hey Dallas, you know how to play? I've seen it in movies but Mama was gonna... no one I knew ever taught me." The Kid set the wooden box down on the coffee table.

Dallas smiled at the sight of it. It was a chess case he had gotten on a job down in Tallahassee years ago. For a while, he had set it up and played against himself, but that shit got boring as hell after a few months. Made him feel like Charlton Heston in *The Omega Man*. Kinda shit crazy fuckers do.

"Yeah, I know how to play. If you want to learn, I'll teach you."

The Kid's face lit up and he nodded without a sound.

"All right." Dallas set his plate down. He opened the case and exposed all the pieces, then picked up the black queen and held it up.

"If someone takes your king, you lose, but this is your most important piece, you hear? Never take your eyes off this piece. It's like..." Dallas sighed and let his arm relax. "Chess is a life lesson." He stood and walked to the fridge, pulling out another cold beer. He paused to twist the cap off and returned to the living room. "You need to think of the thing that's most important in your life." Dallas put a hand on the Kid's shoulder and leaned down to stare him in the eyes. "And what's most important, you keep close to your heart. You never let it leave."

Dallas sat down and took a drink of beer. "So." He stared at the Kid. "You take your eyes off the queen?"

The Kid was meeting his gaze but his eyes darted from the beer Dallas held, to his other empty hand, then the coffee table, and the wooden box. He met Dallas' gaze again. "I..."

Dallas grinned. "You have to keep the queen close to your heart." He raised his beer and motioned to the shirt pocket on the Kid's shirt.

The Kid slowly looked down to his shirt pocket, and then raised a hand to reach inside and pull out the queen. His eyes grew wide as he stared at it. "Dallas, how did you—"

"Don't ever take your eyes off what's close to your heart, Kid. Not ever."

The Kid stared at the queen as if it was a unicorn that had walked into the room and shat rainbow piles on the floor, then he reached out and put it back in the case. He kept staring at the wooden box.

"Dallas?" The Kid's voice was barely a whisper.

"Yeah, Kid?"

"Sometimes... sometimes at night, Mama would talk to me." The sentence hung in the air, heavy and thick, like a thunderhead rolling in.

86

"You mean..." Dallas coughed and cleared his throat. "After?"

"Yeah." The Kid cocked his head and gave a light shrug. "I know, it's not like she *really* did but... sometimes she talked to me."

"What'd she say?" Dallas felt his mouth go desert dry. He grabbed his beer to calm the scorch.

"Different things. She kept saying she was sorry, y' know? Sorry for lettin' things... happen to me. To Darlene. For all the shit Darrell... you know."

Dallas coughed again. "You really think it was her or you think it was that little voice you... we all have in our heads?"

The Kid shifted in the easy chair, then reached for his root beer. "I guess it was just me, right? I mean it's not like she could..."

"Kid, somebody once told me the past don't matter much. It's already happened. The future, well... we can plan our asses off and whatever's gonna happen is gonna happen. But right now, all anybody has is right now. So what're you gonna do with it?"

"Keep it close to your heart like the queen?"

Dallas beamed at him and nodded. "Bingo."

The Kid sipped his root beer and leaned back into the chair as he stared out at nothing. He turned to Dallas and gave a nod. "Thanks, Dallas."

"For what?"

"Everything. Letting me stay with you. Teaching me things." The Kid paused and brought the bottle to his lips but pulled it way without drinking. "For being nice to me." The Kid smiled and it was a big one.

"Anytime, Kid." Dallas reached for his pack of Winstons, lit one, and then started putting the chess pieces out on the coffee table. "Let me show you how to set up the board."

CHAPTER TWENTY NINE

The water was murky and deep. Bits of driftwood and leaves and detritus floated around like wishes in an old well. Small fish darted and swam bullet-quick in the current. She was waiting—arms wide open and welcoming.

"Honey," she said, though no sound was heard but the bubbles that poured from her mouth he somehow interpreted.

"Ma." He called and held his own arms out to her. She floated closer. Her sundress billowing in the water. Fabric undulating like a snake charmer's cobra. Her eyes were black holes—they swallowed everything and things wriggled in there—scaled things that glistened in the darkness. She took hold of his arms and leaned in close to his face. Her mouth opened and he saw her tongue was a great leech. Tiny bubbles flooded his eyes and he heard her voice in his ears. "I tried to set you free, bring you with me to a better place. But you chose the millstone of sin. This world is what you deserve, my son."

"Mama. I didn't mean to keep livin'." He was crying. Under the water it was an invisible act.

"Never said that's what you done." She closed her mouth and her eyes and began to float away. A water-logged angel ascending.

"Don't leave me again, Mama." He called as she became a speck in the distance. "Please don't leave!"

Dallas opened his eyes and realized he wasn't breathing. Well he was, but he was holding the last one hostage in his smoke-scarred lungs. He opened his mouth and let his breath flee. He drew in another and then another and regained a rhythm. He slowly pulled himself to a sitting position and looked at the pack of cigarettes on his bedside table. He looked out the doorway into the hall. He saw the flickering light from the TV and heard the faint whispering of the Kid talking to himself. He knew more about loss than he had let on to the Kid. They were a right pair together.

Dallas thought of that trailer and the Kid's mother moldering away on that sofa. He remembered his own mother smiling up at him as she tied his leg to the cinderblock. She smiled and told him she loved him before she pushed him off the railing. Dallas held his head in his hands and wept as quietly as he could.

CHAPTER THIRTY

Chad wiped the sweat off his forehead and took a drink from his half-gallon jug of sweet tea. He held it in his mouth for a minute before he finally swallowed. The roof on the pool house was coming along and he figured he would be finished up in a few hours. Damned hot work—like he was preparing for Hell kind of hot.

The owner of the place had come by in the morning. Pompous prick, stopping to inspect the new packs of roofing shingles and remind him to make sure to clean up the mess when he was done and not get any debris in the pool.

Chad's gaze took in the landscaped property—bamboo along the far side of the pool, a stone path leading to a Koi pond and gazebo, and the house itself. Two stories of stone with terra cotta tiled roof—the damn place looked like it had been ripped off a hillside in Italy and shipped here rock by rock.

For all I know, it fucking could have been. Chad gave a disgusted laugh. *I oughta piss in the fucking pool.*

What a lifestyle. Chad shook his head and took another cold drink of tea. *Soon, I'll know this kind of life myself. Then it's nothing but expensive liquor and sex in fancy parts of the world that had palm trees. I will never swing a fucking hammer again. Life on easy street. Shit, I can't believe I'm saying this, but I might even ask her to marry me. Eventually.*

Just a few loose ends to tie up first.

The man on the other end of the phone had sounded younger than Chad expected, but that didn't bother him much. Professionals existed at all ages, and Dallas had come highly recommended. *Then again, it's not like there's a fucking Yelp category for hit men reviews, is there?*

A photo. An address. Ten grand.

The first two were easy enough. That last one though...

Slowly, a smile spread over his face. Chad eyeballed the main house again—one big, *beauuuuutiful,* treasure chest just waiting to be raided.

CHAPTER THIRTY ONE

Every single minute of the damned day was as exciting as Christmas Eve, except you weren't sure if Santa was going to come in the morning or decide to push it back a day. Would it happen today? Hell, was it happening now? There was no festively wrapped box to shake or bright bows to fondle.

Morris felt his heart beat faster at the thought and turned on the air conditioning. He sat in his parked car in the company lot and considered the rest of his afternoon—no appointments scheduled.

Maybe I can play a 9-hole game over at Briarwood. Or there's that Thai masseuse—goddamn she was hot—haven't been there in a while. For an extra $20 she'll yank your crank before you leave. He smiled at the thought but it dissipated like childhood. No, probably not. Probably best to have some sort of alibi, just in case.

He reached for a pocket inside his suit jacket and realized he was going for cigarettes that hadn't been there in over 8 years. What the hell? He felt a craving for nicotine wash over him. Morris gripped the steering wheel and let out a slow controlled breath. "Petty was right about the damned waiting."

McCleary's. I'll go have a drink or two at McCleary's. There's always a few local attorneys there at this time of day. Measuring their wallet bulges and comparing their dicks on the bar. Hell, maybe Judge Patterson will be there in his usual corner booth. Oh how amazing would that be to have it go down today, right now, right fucking now, while I'm at McCleary's, being seen by the Judge? A goddamn golden fleece of luck and opportunity.

Morris put the car in drive and headed toward his favorite bar, hoping like hell he would get an early Christmas present today.

CHAPTER THIRTY TWO

Dallas walked inside and set the thick gloves and snake tongs down against the living room wall. He hated the scared squeaks and the pissy old-diaper stink of the mice he fed to the snakes, but the last of them had been dished out. He wanted the rattlers hungry and full of rage when the time was right. Well, hungry at least. Them fuckers seemed to always be raging.

He let out a breath and turned to the Kid, sitting in the lounge chair. The Kid's leg was going for the record.

"Three days, Kid." Dallas sat down on the couch and reached for the Budweiser he'd left on the coffee table earlier. "That's when it goes down."

The Kid looked up from the old issue of *Playboy* he was staring at. His eyes were wide as he peered over the cover with a busty redhead in suspenders and a thong. "Yeah? Okay... do you, y' know, need me to do anything special?" His nonchalant voice definitely needed some work.

"I'll let you know, otherwise just pay attention and learn." Dallas leaned forward and studied the chessboard. He took a drink of beer and motioned with the bottle toward the *Playboy* and grinned. "And don't spank it too much, you'll go blind. How you think my eyesight got to be so damned bad?"

The Kid coughed out a laugh and folded the magazine up as Dallas moved his bishop.

"Check." Dallas eased back on the couch and closed his eyes. *It was all closing in now. Things rushing to a conclusion. One big checkered board with the pieces lining up.*

His eyes still shut, Dallas heard the recliner creak as the Kid edged forward to look at the board.

"You move your knight on the right side and I'll checkmate your ass in two moves."

There was a quiet pause and the chair creaked again as the Kid settled. A little sigh like a ghost.

"Take your time, Kid. Look at the whole board. Study it. Don't trust a single piece in the game. Don't trust anything. Even your teeth bite your tongue once in a while."

The phone in his pocket buzzed and Dallas pulled it out. "Yeah."

"Heads up on a client referral. He was asking around for a travel agent." Dallas recognized Henry's voice with his tired, labored breathing.

"That's great news as we love to serve. Was the client in a rush to get on vacation?"

"I think so. He was trying to squeeze a trip in pretty soon."

"Okay. You refer him to our mobile office or headquarters?"

There was a snicker on the other end. Dallas heard Darlene's voice yelling about something in the background.

"Headquarters."

"Okay. Thank you and please expect a referral fee after the

client's vacation booking is confirmed."

Dallas flipped his phone shut.

The Kid was staring at the board like he was waiting for water to boil but he glanced at Dallas. "All good?"

"Might have another possible project. Busiest damn time I've had in months. Guy's supposed to call the landline."

The Kid nodded and he turned back to study the board. His right hand started to flex open and closed and his leg was threatening to tear free at the hip and bounce right out the fucking door.

CHAPTER THIRTY THREE

Chad sat in the parking lot of his workshop with the air conditioning running in his pickup. The truck was a chrysalis of cigarette smoke and loud music. Black Flag. Chad squinted and looked at the cash he'd gotten for the carload of goods he'd separated from Pool House Asshole. That fucking guy left for Aruba and wouldn't be back for three weeks. Plenty of time for Chad to get things done and be gone.

He'd been smart enough to drive over the state line to foist them off. He got close to $4000 for the televisions, computers, the silver and china and all that jewelry. It wasn't what he needed but it was a start. He had some jobs he'd yet to collect on and might come close to matching what he had now, especially if he laid on the pouting act and guilted them for not paying at job's end.

Funny thing that poor folks, or folks who're just scraping by, are more likely to pay you the day you finish the job or maybe even up front. But the rich, they're so high on their own ass wind, so caught up in being their own satellites that they don't pay you until you come sniffing. Like, they get off on seeing you beg for something rightfully owed. Bastards one and all. Maybe Dallas, young as he sounded, would let him pay half up front and half after it was done. I mean, a lot of private contractors deal that way.

Chad picked up the cell from the passenger seat and dialed

Victoria.

"Where is that girl?" He sighed as the phone belched a steady unanswered ringing into his ear. *She was supposed to be here twenty minutes ago. I have shit to do!*

He closed it and tossed it back behind the seat among the CD cases and empty water bottles. He sucked the last blood from his cigarette and dropped it in the paper cup serving as an ashtray and threw the truck in reverse. Turning to look in his driver's side mirror, Chad slammed his brakes as a dark blue sedan angled to a stop behind him.

"What the fuck?" He put the shifter back in park and stepped out. The door to the sedan swung open and the driver got out. Big man, a good four inches taller than Chad and a helluva lot wider, and he didn't hesitate to step from behind his door. Chad noticed he had a hand to his waist, resting on the grip of a pistol. Chad's stomach lurched a little.

"How ya doin'?" The man grinned and flipped open a leather case, showing credentials and a badge flashed in the sun. "Got a minute?" The man's smile grew wider.

CHAPTER THIRTY FOUR

That tricky motherfucker! Victoria gripped the steering wheel and shook it in rage. She felt like screaming. Her phone rang as it rested in the center console and she glanced at it, praying in that split second it was Dallas calling, telling her the job was completed, that it hadn't gone smoothly and he'd been forced to bludgeon the man to death with a ball peen hammer. But no, it was Chad again, for the third time in the last half hour.

"I'm on my way, dumbass!" Victoria yelled at her phone and looked at the small black box with the blinking green light sitting on her passenger seat.

How fucking long has this been on my car? Tracking my every goddamn move. Oh this was going to play out lovely in court, wasn't it? Screw it. Didn't prove anything. Was probably inadmissible, right? HAD to be! That shifty fuck.

"Fuuuuuuuucccckkkk!" She wondered when Morris had put it there. He had his car in the shop a week or so ago and borrowed hers. *Was it then? Motherfucker!*

Victoria turned left onto Vansant Drive and pulled to the right side of the street, coming to a stop. She always parked at least a half a block away, whether it was his apartment or his business. And now, she glanced at the device again, I'm guessing parking a distance away was a pretty good strategy if things... WHEN things end up in court. She parked and checked herself in the mirror. Mascara was a little blurry from frustration tears. *Doesn't matter. Chad always makes my eyes water during sex anyway. He probably won't even notice.*

Victoria took several steps on the sidewalk and stopped. A midnight blue, unmarked cruiser ran into Chad's gravel lot and parked behind his truck, blocking him in. Chad got out of his truck, and the man stepped free of the cruiser. He moved with intent, holding an arm out toward Chad as if to present something. She saw the sunlight glint off of metal. *Oh shit!*

What the hell was a cop doing with Chad? Victoria stepped backward toward her car, leaning on the roof, but keeping an eye on the two men. Chad waved the man on and both of them went inside his office workshop. She watched the sign hanging on the front door flip sides and knew he had turned it to CLOSED.

Whatever this is, it's not good. She chewed her lip and pressed the key fob to unlock her car. As Victoria got into the driver's seat, she stopped herself and stared at the all-knowing blinking box on the passenger seat. She glanced back at the parked cop car and the stress on her face gave way, the rainclouds fading to clear skies again. She grabbed the box from the seat and started walking. Her eyes never left the door to Chad's shop. The window shades were down and there was no sound of movement. She neared the blue car and knelt as she reached under the back wheel well and attached the small box to the frame. She stayed low and sort of backwards crab-walked across the street and into the masking shade of the trees that lined it. She stood and briskly ate up the distance back to her car.

"Play with me, motherfucker? Well let's see how you like this game."

CHAPTER THIRTY FIVE

Something was up with the Kid. Dallas couldn't quite put his finger on it but he was damn certain the boy was squirrelier than usual.

"Another coffee?" The young waitress asked, a carafe poised to refill his mug.

"Sure." Dallas smiled at her. "May I get an order of bacon and sausage to go too, please?"

"You certainly may." She gave him a bright smile. "Be right back with it." She headed toward the kitchen and Dallas did his usual, admiring her caboose in her tight-fitting outfit.

He took a gulp of the black coffee and thought about the Kid. He *should* be sleeping on the couch right now but when Dallas got up, he had still been awake, watching some damned infomercial about a vacuum. Dallas put on his shoes and told him he needed to run out for more smokes and some raisin bran.

It wasn't a complete lie.

The Kid was like a puppy—all heart and need to be petted and have a little affectionate scratch under the chin to keep him loyal. "At least he don't shit on the floor." He mumbled, lost in thought as the waitress appeared like a specter and sat the grease-stained bag before him.

"That's usually a deal breaker for me too."

"What?" He said, awkwardly aware he must have spoken but not sure at all what he'd said.

"Not shitting on the floor. Weirdoes might dig that in the big city but I'm a good ol' gal." She gave him her sincere, winning smile again.

"Heh. I was talking about my dog. Thinking out loud."

"What kind is he? Don't mind my askin'?"

"Oh, he's just a mutt. A rescue." He watched her features glow as she smiled.

"That's great."

"Yeah, why get something new when there's good ones out there that need the love and appreciation, right?" Dallas stood and pulled a small wad of bills from his pocket. He peeled off a twenty and laid it on the table in front of the girl. "Keep the change, darlin'. And thanks again."

"Thank you. And hug that dog for me."

Dallas did not reply and walked out the door.

CHAPTER THIRTY SIX

The Kid was supposed to be sleeping. He was straight up ordered to lay the fuck down and close his damned eyes by Dallas before he left. He hadn't slept for days, outside of an hour here or there. He was a live wire. Excitement surged through him like a Tesla coil. He laid on the couch and listened to the four hundred thoughts jockeying for space in a head with only room for three hundred and fourteen of them.

As soon as Dallas had pulled out this morning, the Kid had run to the old yellow phone on the kitchen wall. He pinched the end of the cord that stretched to the jack in the baseboard and pushed it into place, hearing the click as he did. He had unplugged it a day ago, scared his client would call back and Dallas would pick up. Guilt over this had added to the list of things keeping him from sleep.

He paced the living room, keeping his gaze trained out the front windows as he murmured to himself. "Greg Evigan starred as Billie Joe BJ McKay, a freelance trucker. He drove a red and white Kenworth K-100 Aerodyne with his pet chimpanzee Bear. BJ named the chimp after Coach Bryan of—"

The wall phone rang and the Kid leaped across the room, damn near ripping it from the wall as he grabbed it. "Yeah."

"This uh... Dallas? I've been trying to get ahold of you. Fucking the wife of a man—"

"This is him." The Kid could feel adrenaline course through his chest and flow down through his legs. "You have the money and information?"

There was hesitation on the other end of the line, a breath and the sound of someone licking dry lips. "I have all of that. Photograph. Address. Full payment."

Excitement slammed through the Kid's veins. *Is this how Dallas feels every job? Holy shit!* "Good. Tonight at eleven o'clock. You remember where?"

"Yeah."

"Good. Don't call back." The Kid hung the phone up and almost staggered back to the couch. He felt almost drunk. It reminded him of the time Mama and Darrell had gone on a bender and left him to fend for himself so he ate two boxes of Froot Loops and a box of Apple Jacks and damn near had himself in a sugar coma.

He couldn't wait to take the Chad job. He'd make Dallas so proud. Show him he was a normal person. "I'll be a real boy," he said in his best Pinocchio voice. The excitement in his veins was leaving as quickly as it had arrived, but the Kid could feel music playing over the sound of the engine as Dallas pulled up to the house. Lady Gaga. That old man was an odd duck for sure. The Kid closed his eyes and calmed himself counting, and by the time Dallas got inside, he was asleep. Just like a real boy.

CHAPTER THIRTY SEVEN

"Whatcha want, Weasel? Ahh, sorry, I mean Wesley."

The voice on the line was gravelly and rough. *Battered as an old tin can on the roadside,* Wesley thought. *A job like this, you rub against used goods all day long. Can't ever scrub this shit off.*

"Well if it isn't my little blackbird! My little blackbird Benny. Now that's no way to say hello to a friend, now is it?"

"Friend, my ass. I ask again, whatcha after?"

Wesley gripped his phone and clenched his jaw. It had become very clear to him, quite recently, that he no longer had the patience for bullshit. If he was honest, that reservoir had been pretty fucking shallow to begin with. "Don't get uppity with me. You think it's easy getting your boys out of that pile of shit they were in upstate? Three kilos and unregistered weapons charges. You think that just gets brushed away?"

"Don't mean I gotta crawl through this phone and slobber your knob. What. Do. You. Want?"

Gritting his teeth, Wesley felt his molars start to ache. "Keep testing me you old spook, and see what the fuck happens. I'll have your boys buried so far under concrete and steel bars they'll never see the light of day unless it's to take it up the ass by some of the Aryan brotherhood or long neck some guard's pecker."

Wesley heard nothing but the sound of heavy breathing and the soft whistle of oxygen through plastic tubing.

"I'm not testing you, Wesley. And I know my boys are up against some heavy shit. I told you I'd give you what you want if I get what I want. All this bullshit might go sideways but I damn well don't give a shit. Hell, from where I'm at, sideways is a lot like up. I want my boys cleared and free no matter what."

"No matter what? What, you think you're calling the shots—"

"Now *you* listen to *me*, you fuckin' cracker. Ain't a man in my goddamn family scared of doin' time. If they go in, they won't be the first or the last. Get me the goddamn paperwork. Signed."

There was coughing on the other end, deep and rattling and thick with phlegm. The coughing ended with a rough hawking noise from the man's throat. It sounds like someone tenderizing raw meat.

"Okay Benny. I'll get the paperwork for you. You just sing to me like the little blackbird you are if you hear something. You know how the song goes. You know how it is..."

Another clearing of a throat and the sound of thick mucus being spit out. "Yeah, Wesley. I know how it is, all right."

"So, tell me what you know about a shit stain named Dallas Livingston?"

The tired wheeze on the other end paused for a second that marched like hours.

"I don't know any—"

"Stop, Benniford. Right there. I know that a scumfuck spade like you would know a scumfuck cracker such as he. Probably even fucked once or twice. But don't try fuckin' *me* right now. Tell me what you know."

CHAPTER THIRTY EIGHT

Benny managed to get the receiver back to its cradle and then he sat in the darkness of the trailer. Through the living room windows, he could see the pinpoint glow of lightning bugs across the field behind the house. The television was off in the living room so it was calm and quiet save for the rhythmic wheezing of his lungs and the dull fucking thump of the car speakers outside as the boys listened to their gangsta shit. The oxygen felt cool against his nostrils.

Benny had a feeling and it wasn't a good one. Weren't nothin' felt as heavy and rough as betrayal.

Gramma had always told him the only strong feelings are bad ones. Good ones were frail as moths and just as dusty. The older he got the righter she seemed to be. He closed his eyes and listened as a slow drizzle began to fall outside. He hoped it was a cleansing rain although he was entirely certain there wasn't enough water to wash his soul.

CHAPTER THIRTY NINE

"You got a hot date or something, Kid?" Dallas crushed his butt into the ashtray on the chair arm and leaned a little to pick up the bottle beside him.

"What do you mean?"

"Well, I've caught you looking at the clock no less than ten times in the last ten minutes. That leg is logging the fucking miles and you've not been worth a shit for conversation all evening. So I'm just inquiring as to what's up?"

"Oh. Um... Darlene wants me to meet her when she gets off work. She said we needed to talk about things and I'm excited and scared at the same time." The Kid was surprised with how easily the lie slipped from his lips.

"Well, maybe you ought to. We tied up the other ends for you, boy. Talking things out with her might be all that's left to do and then you'd be free." Dallas took a pull on his beer and sat the bottle on the floor beside him. "You want me to take you over there and wait with you?"

"No, I'm fine. It's only down the road and the moon's a big full one. It stopped raining."

"That's good as I'm in no shape to drive." Dallas stood up from the chair and faltered a little, having to steady himself on the arm.

"Shit, I might not be in any shape to get back to bed." He laughed and the Kid reached out to help him balance.

"I'm good, son. I just didn't eat much today and then played the genius and drank too many. That's bad math."

"Lock up when you leave. You know where the extra is outside to get back in." Dallas dropped his empty in the blue bin by the door and turned to go back down the hall. The Kid looked at the clock again and shook the floor. "Be careful while walking and pay attention. I don't want you run over like a fucking polecat."

"Okay, Dallas. Wait, what's a polecat?"

"Another name for a skunk. A polecat. Stinkpussy. Speaking of which, why don't you slap that hot piece sister of yours on the ass from me." He followed that with a throaty chuckle and the Kid smiled but it was not an easy one.

"I won't do that."

"Was a joke, Kid. Apparently not a very good one. I sometimes lose objectivity when I'm drunk."

"Oh."

"I'm going to bed. Remember what I said and I'll see you in the morning, and if my head isn't hollering, we'll go for breakfast."

"Bacon and sausage?"

"What else could there possibly be?"

"I think I'd like to try grits one day. What are they anyway?"

"Pulverized corn."

"Wow. I'd definitely like to try grits then."

"Kid, you are truly one of a kind." Dallas smiled and clapped the boy's shoulder before turning back the hall.

"'Night, Dallas."

"Goodnight, Kid." Dallas made it to his room and closed the door.

The Kid went back to watching the clock and muttering to himself under his breath, mainly about how bad he felt lying to the only person who ever truly gave a shit about him until the lucid thoughts were torpedoed by trivial nonsense and oddly fired synapses.

CHAPTER FORTY

Dallas was stone cold sober.

His hand automatically went for the bedroom light switch before his mind caught it and ordered it to stop. He shuffled to the bed and sat down, shifting enough to make the springs squeak for added affect. He would sit tight and wait until he heard the Kid leave and then he'd follow him and see what was going on.

If there was one thing The Kid couldn't do, it was lie. It was like a nervous man trying to veil the fact he'd farted in church. Dallas laid back and stared at the ceiling, very glad he'd never regaled the boy with any of the stories from his younger acting days. He wished he could light up a smoke. He side-glanced at the old flip number clock on the dresser. It was 10:23pm.

Kid, what the fuck are you up to?

He sat in the dark, in the quiet, with only the noise of his mind and the cricket song seeping in through the window to keep him company.

CHAPTER FORTY ONE

"It's real fuckin' simple. You drive up, get out of your car, and hand him the envelope with the information, got it?"

Chad nodded silently.

"You fuckin' got it or what?" Wesley held his hands out toward Chad to emphasize his words.

"I said I got it, okay?" This cop was a real power tripping asshole. On top of that he seemed like he was coked the fuck out of his mind. He reminded Chad of the tweakers he ran with in his younger days. The big man was all agitation and barely coiled anger. To say the cop made him uneasy would be a Staten Island-sized understatement. Chad ran a hand back over his head. He was sweating and it wasn't because the shop air conditioning was on the fritz again.

"Okay, then." Wesley put his hands down to his sides. "Chrissakes, speak and don't be such a Helen fuckin' Keller." He reached for a black bag, not much larger than a loaf of bread. "You confirm, out loud with him, what you're paying him for and what you expect him to do for this money. I want that on tape, loud and clear."

He's been here for four goddamn hours asking questions. Has he met Dallas in person or just talked on the phone? He asked that about eight times already.

Chad had considered lying about this, but in the end, he figured it would all come out anyway. He told him the truth and recounted how he had been having a few drinks over at the Knuckle Bucket and things had come up. The bouncer, or manager, or whatever-the-fuck-he-was—Henry—had given him the name and number.

Chad wiped the sweat from his forehead with his hand, and then on his pants. "And that's it?"

"For now."

Chad shook his head and stared out the window of his workshop. His inner voice was working him over like a thug. *Fucking hell. How the hell did I wind up here over a piece of cooze? No, it was more than that... it was the damned money, too. Idiot. Goddamned idiot! And Officer Dickhead is relentless. I need a drink.*

Wesley stood up from the dirty office chair and stared at Chad. His expression changed from a furrowed brow to gentle concern. He frowned slightly, and spoke with a soft, lowered voice. "Look man, this... is a lot. I haven't been thinking of what you're going through at all. We're putting you in a highly... stressful situation. I'm not a monster, brother. I have a heart."

Chad picked up a foam cup of cold coffee and took a sip. He nodded back at the officer. "Yeah, it is. I mean, I'm not—"

Wesley slammed a fist down on the table and leaned in toward Chad with a grimace smeared over his face as he yelled. "You fucking hired someone to kill the husband of your slutty girlfriend. You think I give a *shiiiiit* what kinda stress you're under, motherfucker? You're my bitch until I say otherwise, so get used to it!" He pushed on the table, hard, then turned and took a few steps away, staring out the front window of the workshop. The blinds were still drawn so this was purely for show.

The audio mic taped to his chest itched and Chad wanted to rip it off his skin. *Why in the fuck did I do this? Dad used to say men went pussymad at times. Guess this is what he meant.* He bit his lip, thought about drinking the rest of the coffee, but pushed the cup away from him instead.

"It goes step by step. One foot in front of the other." The officer's voice was calmer now. "Get the audio. Hand over the money. Get him to say what you're paying him for and leave." He turned to face Chad again. "Three things. A, b, three. Think you can handle that?"

Chad's stomach was in knots. He swallowed hard, and then looked up at the man. "Yeah, I think I can handle that."

"You fuckin' better."

Chapter Forty Two

Victoria chewed the insides of her cheeks when she was agitated and right now she could taste the faintest dead penny flavor inside her mouth. She spat a small wad of pink foamy saliva onto the carpet. She didn't care.

She walked out onto the patio, took a deep breath of fresh air, and sat down at the cast iron café table. Swirls of uncertainty flowed through her.

What the hell was a cop doing with Chad? I mean, I know him, but I don't really know him. I've tasted his dick and let him use me like a shake 'n bake bag but what else do I know? He's lived in town for the past six years, has a kid he doesn't talk to over in Tennessee or maybe it was South Carolina. Got into some trouble after high school dealing meth and... and... goddamn it! I don't even know his fucking middle name!

She sipped from the glass of chardonnay, then put it back to her lips and drank several swallows. It set her mouth on fire with stinging pain, but she gulped it down anyway. She looked out over her backyard, stretching beyond the deck in all its lush greenery. The landscaping. *So... tidy. Everything in its place. Every leaf nipped and trimmed and manicured. Have to keep up appearances.*

Maybe Chad was dealing again and hadn't told me. I'm in his phone. Jesus Fuck! I'm in his goddamn phone!

She reached for her phone from the table. Last she had heard from him was six hours ago, right before she almost walked into the hornet's nest happening at his workshop.

Victoria stiffened. The tracker. *Oh-my-fucking-god, the tracker. Was it the cops? Maybe it wasn't Morris who put it on her car. Was it the cops, trying to see how she and Chad interacted?* Her stomach dropped like an elevator in a disaster movie.

Fuck! FUCK FUCK FUCKFUCKFUCKFUCK!

She stood and threw the wine glass as far as she could into the backyard. She bent over the deck railing and let out a wavering breath to try and collect herself. This was not good.

Not good at all.

CHAPTER FORTY THREE

Dallas heard the thin metallic clicking of the kitchen door as it opened and closed. He waited a three count, and then went to his bedroom window to see the Kid walking down the short gravel patch serving as the driveway. Dallas waited until he saw the Kid turn right at the road and stepped from his bedroom.

The television was still on in the living room and a tray from a TV dinner was on the coffee table beside the electronic tablet.

He shook his head. The boy was a stickler for cleaning up after himself. "Kid, I don't know what kinda shit you're messin' with, but I'm sure it's nothin' good to have you behavin' like this."

Dallas shrugged his jacket on and grabbed his keys. For the first time in a long time, he thought of his pistol tucked away back in his bedroom. He hated the damn things. Blunt, idiotic tools. Lazy. Any old fool could use one.

But right then it crossed his mind and made him realize he feared for whatever the Kid was mixed up in. What bothered him more was how he couldn't exactly put his finger on *why*.

Dallas paused in his living room, keys in hand, considering, and then reached down to grab the remote to turn the television off. He glanced at the tablet. The Kid hadn't even told him what the Missus had been up to with her day like he was supposed to be doing.

He sat down, tossed his keys on the table and hit the power

button for the tablet. There were two jobs going on right now, and complicated ones at that. The screen of the tablet lit up and Dallas pulled up tracking history. Mrs. Morris had been a busy little beaver for a while, traveling here and there, but today wasn't active at all. He tapped a finger on a pin on the map and it pulled up a time slot. Damn near 5 hours at a location in town.

Hmmm. I'll have to check on that shit. Hair, nails, and a happy ending massage don't take that long. Something's off.

Dallas tapped the tracker again, bringing it current. The green dot appeared on screen and was on the move out of town and heading west.

The fucking Kid lied. Goddamn it.

Dallas stood up again, gripping the tablet. He had other things to focus on right now, goddamn it, and worrying what the Kid was getting into wasn't part of it. Shouldn't be.

But it was. Dallas gritted his teeth. *A soft spot for sure. I goddamn well know better.*

He grabbed the pillow the Kid had been using and shook the pillowcase free. He stuffed it into his pocket like a pair of panties on prom night.

He reached inside his jacket for his cigarettes and shook one loose, cursed himself for doing it out of habit when he was frustrated and tucked it back into the pack. Now he felt like an idiot just standing there in his living room.

"Fuck it!" Dallas pulled the smoke free again and lit it, grabbing the reptile tongs on his way out the door.

CHAPTER FORTY FOUR

The Kid walked slower as he approached the acre haunted by the ashes of his shitbox trailer. He could still smell the smoke it bled as it died. He scanned the perimeter of hedges and trees and realized how eerie it was. He looked at his watch and saw he was a few minutes early. He stopped at the edge of the road beneath the streetlight, and jammed his hands further into his pockets. He could hear his heart beating like voodoo drums.

"Dallas?" he heard the voice clear in the darkness and the Kid could make out the shape of a truck parked along the roadside. The Kid watched a man walking toward him, stepping into the dull glow of the streetlight. He was lean and tall. His hair was long and dirty blonde. His beard matched. The Kid swallowed hard.

"Yeah." The man was walking up on him fast. The Kid was getting nervous. His periphery was filled with movement and shadows. "You're Chad?"

"Yes. Here's the information you asked for." The man held out a hand that held a large thick envelope with a smaller one on top. "The little one is the info and the big one is your money."

"Okay." the Kid reached out and grasped it. He paused. *What was that noise? It sounded like maracas in a far away room.*

"You know what the money's for?" Chad asked, staring the Kid right in the eyes. His face shone with sweat. The Kid swallowed again.

"Sure, I do." He tried to take the envelopes.

Chad held them tight. "Say it."

"What?" The Kid croaked.

"Tell me again what I'm paying you for." Chad spoke slowly and enunciated every syllable.

The Kid stared as a shadow moved in quickly from somewhere behind Chad. As the pillowcase was pulled over the man's head and the sound of muffled rattling and hissing grew louder. Then shadow man pushed Chad aside and grabbed the Kid by the arm turning him toward the woods.

"Run, Kid! Move!"

The Kid's eyes grew as recognition set in but Dallas held up a finger to his lips. Dallas hunkered into a crouch and started to hoof it when he heard a man yell behind him.

"Stop or I will damn well shoot!"

CHAPTER FORTY FIVE

Dallas turned and saw a man standing by a jumble of scorched aluminum, his piece drawn and leveled at him. On the ground, Chad was writhing like the snake that was no doubt perforating his neck and face. The muffled wailing was horrific. The man with the gun took steps towards Chad, never taking his eyes or aim from Dallas. He kicked the pillowcase and the rattling started again.

The cop pulled the gun sharply and fired. The rattling and hissing stopped. All was still. "A fucking snake? Really?"

Dallas shrugged and looked off to the right. He thought he saw movement along the tree line. That fucking Kid. "You got me. What else do you need?"

"I knew that fucking kid wasn't Dallas. I didn't know who Dallas really was but a gawky nut-job kid who talks to himself definitely wasn't the bull's-eye there."

"He's nothing to concern yourself with. Just a decoy. You got your prize."

"That I do."

Chad lurched to his feet and pulled the bloody pillowcase from his head.

The officer saw the snake-bit eyeball oozing down the man's cheek—a small jellyfish on a reddening beach—and the swollen melon of a head teetering on his scrawny neck. A thick froth dripped from his engorged lips. Wesley opened his mouth and a wild laugh flew from it. He looked at Dallas. "Rattlesnake," he cackled. "You take the fuckin' cake, my friend."

Dallas bolted towards the tree line and moved like a man half his age. The cop turned with the intent of pursuit.

That was when the Escalade swerved into the yard and two black men jumped out with guns at the ready. The back door opened and Benny dragged his bulk out and waddled toward him, portable tank swaying like an extra limb.

"Weasel. I swear you could fuck up a wet dream." He wheezed and released a soft chuckle.

Chad fell to his knees and clawed at his rapidly closing windpipe. Wesley shot Chad in the face without even looking at him and as soon as the man fell he turned on Benny and the boys. "It's like you fuckers got a stereotype checklist in your wallets—a fuckin' Escalade? Check! And them fucking rims? My lands." Wesley smiled, then winced and leaned forward a little. It was obvious he was no longer accustomed to this level of physical assertion.

"He got away. Let's get after 'em fellas, if you want that"Get Outta Jail Free" card." Wesley stood and wiped his forehead on his sleeve.

"You boys go with him, I need to get my wheels." Benny leaned into the vehicle and hit the button to lower the hydraulic platform on the back. On it, his red mobility scooter shined like a bloodstain in the moonlight.

CHAPTER FORTY SIX

"Kid?" Dallas shout-whispered in the darkness of the woods.

There was no answer but the rustle of leaves and branches in the breeze.

"Goddammit, Kid!" He tried again.

Nothing. More wind tongue whispers.

"I'm not mad at you." He lied. "Not really. Just want you safe."

There was a loud crack as something of weight stepped on a branch, followed by the shushing crunch of footfalls on leaves. A shadow moved in from his left and Dallas turned quickly and saw the Kid, pale as the moon in the dim. He'd been crying and his cheeks were glassy with tears.

"Awww, Kid." Dallas wrapped his arms around the boy and drew him close. "You okay?"

"I'm sorry, Dallas." That was all. That was enough. They stood there in the night woods for several minutes before they moved on.

CHAPTER FORTY SEVEN

Victoria pulled the sliding glass door and stepped inside as someone moved past the entrance.

"Oh Jesus!" Victoria chuckled to herself and put her head down. "Consuela, you scared the sh... you scared me." She smiled at the maid. "Wasn't expecting you this late."

"I'm sorry, Mrs. Mussey. I didn't mean to. I told Mr. Mussey I'd stop by after my son's ballgame to finish the dusting and bathrooms. I'll come back day after tomorrow to do the usual." Consuela smiled back but had an expression of concern on her face. Of fear.

"It's okay. Really." Victoria continued smiling a bit longer than normal to put her at ease. Consuela had been their maid for the past two years and was a good one. Attention to detail. The little things really did matter.

The maid went about her business in the bathrooms and reappeared in the living room, putting a feather duster to work behind the pictures on the mantel. She pulling a bottle of cleaner from her work bucket to spray the fireplace glass. She was thorough.

Victoria watched her as she worked. Consuela was from Columbia. If she had to guess, the woman was in her early 30s at most. Victoria thought Consuela had a three-year-old son, and if she had, her body had bounced back nicely. *Tight figure beneath the gray maid outfit. High cheekbones and bright smile. Nice legs. Ample breasts. Hair pulled back in a jet-black ponytail.*

"Consuela?"

"Yes, Mrs. Mussey?"

Victoria walked toward the couch and sat down. "Can I ask you something? And be honest with me. I won't get mad, no matter what your answer is. But be honest, okay?"

The maid, gripping the duster, stood in front of the fireplace and nodded at her. Her mouth a straight line.

"My husband... has he..." Victoria crossed her legs and regretted throwing the glass of chardonnay away. She longed for another already. "Has my husband ever done anything... has he ever acted inappropriately toward you in any way?"

Consuela looked down at the feather duster she held, then her gaze rose to meet Victoria. "No. Never."

"It's okay if he has. I mean... it's not okay, but it's okay to tell me."

The woman looked downward and seemed to ponder the question, then met her eyes again. "No, Mrs. Mussey. Your husband, he has always been nice to me. Nothing out of line."

Victoria stared at her, holding her gaze for a moment, studying her expression. She was telling the truth. "Okay. Thank you."

The maid smiled and nodded and lifted her cleaning bucket. "I'll be back on Thursday. You have a good night Mrs. Mussey. I'm sorry again for startling you." She started to walk toward the front door.

"Consuela?"

"Yes?"

"You're doing a great job here. You always have."

The woman tilted her head slightly and for a moment, Victoria felt she was looking at her not as a client but as a fellow woman for the very first time. "Are you okay, Mrs. Mussey?"

Victoria opened her mouth to speak and then closed it. She realized it had been a very long time since anyone had actually asked her that, honestly caring about what her reply may be. "I will be."

Consuela gave another curt nod, crossed the space towards the door and left. Victoria walked toward the kitchen, got another glass, and poured a fresh chardonnay. She heard the front door open once and shut and then the sounds repeated. The noise of keys tossed on the foyer table.

She drank from the glass as she went back to the living room and sat down on the couch as Morris came up the steps. "Hey."

"Hey." He shrugged off his suit jacket, draped it over the back of the chair beside him and started down the hall.

"You hungry? I can order something."

Morris paused, holding his briefcase in one hand and the suit jacket in the other. "No. No, I'm good." He actually looked confused by her offer.

His expression is always so cold lately and, Victoria thought, *who can blame him? It's a game. Both of us know things are sliding into a pile of shit. It was a matter of who's going to win the game at the end. Still, I have to know what angles he's playing.*

She smiled at him and set her wine glass on the coffee table, then stood and walked to him.

"If you don't have plans, I was thinking maybe we could..." She slid her hand around his waist and turned her head so she could get closer to his neck. "Maybe drink too much wine and get naked in the hot tub like we used to." She planted a soft kiss on the side of his neck.

He grunted but didn't pull away, and Victoria noticed a slight smirk on his face. "What do you say?"

"That... sounds great but I have to... I have to go meet Reynolds later. Going over some paperwork. It's important."

Victoria pouted her lips. "That's too bad. I got a Brazilian yesterday." She trailed her index finger along the line of his jaw and over his lips. "Your loss."

"Rain check?" Morris leaned forward and kissed her forehead. His lips were dry and cracked.

She raised her eyebrows and shrugged slightly, and let him go. Morris walked on toward the bedroom and Victoria moved back to her wine.

The thought of fucking him again repulsed her but she had to get a reaction from him. *Morris is a lying cheating prick, but let's be honest, he's not part of any brain trust. Probably couldn't spell Mensa let alone hope for membership. The tracker on my car wasn't put there by his hand. Our marriage is going in the dumpster and we both know it, but Morris isn't following my every move. That leaves that asshole cop and the line from him leads straight to one other person.*

Victoria sat back and drank a healthy swallow of wine, emptying the glass. *Chad, you dumb son of a bitch, what have you gotten me into?*

Chapter Forty Eight

Dallas heard the unskilled steps in the distance, trying to be quiet as they stepped in the woods. The moonlight shone down through the overhead branches, turning everything shades of gray and silver.

"Kid, come with me." He whispered his words and stepped, slowly, toward a fallen tree as big round as his waist. "Lay down here now. No time for bullshit, just listen to me."

The Kid did as he was told and straightened out next to the log and Dallas knelt and started scooping dry leaves and twigs over him. "Stay here. Keep out of sight and stay put for as long as you can. When you think, *no*, when you *know* the coast is clear, head to the Knuckle Bucket and tell your uncle Skeeter what's going on."

"Dallas, I—"

"I said no time for bullshit. Not now." He brushed the leaves over the Kid's legs and chest and pulled some sticks over his face, still streaked with tears. Dallas dug his hands in the loose dirt and rubbed them over the boy's dampened face.

"I'm sorry."

"I know, Kid. I know."

Dallas crouched, listening. Two of them off to his left. Deer hunters, they would never be. If he weren't so scared he'd be able to imagine this whole fucking fiasco to the tune of *Yakety Sax*. He rose and started picking his footsteps to the right, trying to hit moss or bare dirt whenever he could.

Eighty feet out, Dallas ducked beneath the branches of a tall pine tree, the blanket of needles beneath it as soft and quiet as an old lady's quilt. He put his hands on the trunk, feeling the sticky sap beneath his palms. People rarely looked up when they were searching. That was a fact. Dallas put his hands around the lowest branch he could grab and put a foot on the tree trunk and began to heave himself upward.

A shiny pistol barrel appeared out of nowhere, trained right on his face.

"Don't fucking move."

CHAPTER FORTY NINE

The Kid shut his eyes tight but they still stung with tears.

What did I do? Jesus Christ, what did I do? I didn't mean it, Dallas. I didn't mean to.

He heard yelling in the distance but couldn't make out the words. Things were crawling on his arms but he didn't slap them away. He didn't move, except for his fingers, which had a mind of their own. Other than some light from the moon, it was pretty dark. He had always hated the dark. It reminded him of being a little kid. Bad things always happened in the dark.

Actors, last names.

A is for Alan Alda. B is for Matthew Broderick. C is for Tom Cruise. D is for—

A gunshot roared out from the hill below, the noise rolling up into the woods, washing over him like a bad dream. The words in his mind dove for cover and stifled the gasp rushing behind them.

The Kid's tears rolled down the sides of his face and trickled down his neck. The looming forest around him was his only embrace. He swallowed every sob as quietly as he could. Somewhere above him things flitted in the night.

CHAPTER FIFTY

Wesley nudged him in the back with the gun barrel as he marched out onto the road. "Any time you feel like running, you go for it."

"How exactly does one decide on a professional career of being a prick? I mean, clearly you're a natural at it, but did you have training as well or—"

"You better keep that fucking sense of humor where you're going. You're gonna need it."

Benny's grandsons walked down the field from the forest line. Wesley had yelled at them from the woods that he had Dallas. Part of him wanted to put a bullet in him right there and end it. Just blow his damned brains out in the woods and leave his body to rot.

Pieces of shit like this don't deserve a fair trial and due justice. He cast a glance at Benny's boys loping down the hill. *I oughta just shoot them too.*

Benny's scooter came bursting out of the copse of trees as well, that electric whir foreign and out of place. Wesley watched as he came riding down the hillside, seesawing over rocks and all of the other bumps in the dirt. He hit the base of the hill and almost upended in the ditch, then evened out on the gravel. He beamed at Wesley like he'd just won the fucking Daytona 500.

Wesley shook his head and spoke under his breath. "Fucking spook." He saw Dallas turn to look at the hillside and for a moment he paused in his march, then kept going forward again.

When they reached his cruiser, Wesley jammed his pistol in Dallas' back again. "Down on your knees."

"I'll bet you say that to all the church boys, don't you?" Dallas smiled like they told you to do on picture day in elementary school.

Wesley slammed him against the side of the car and reached onto the driver's seat to grab his cuffs, never taking the barrel of his gun off Dallas as he did.

"Well, well. Dudley Do Right got his man. Looks like you ain't a pure fuck up after all." Benny pulled up on his scooter and came to a stop in the middle of the road. A sawed-off shotgun rested on the steering column. Benny adjusted his oxygen tubing under his nose as his grandsons came walking up, pistols gleaming in the moonlight. "American hero and all that honky shit."

"That's right, old man." Wesley undid one side of the handcuffs and reached toward Dallas' left arm.

"Got those papers for my grandsons yet?"

Wesley pressed his pistol barrel against Dallas' spine and turned toward Benny. "I got your fucking paperwork, okay? It's being over-nighted to you. You'll have to sign for it in the morning." The handcuff dangled from his hand and he motioned to the two men. "They're off the hook, proud members of society again. But they fuck up again, and being reprehensible black trash like they are, we know it's all but *guaranfuckingteed,* they're going down hard, you hear?"

Dallas turned his head to look at Benny. "You're kidding me, right? You made a fuckin' deal with this prick? Seriously? Send me up the river to save your grandsons?"

Benny shrugged and leaned back against the scooter seat. "We known each other a long time, Dally. You know how this game is. Don't trust anybody. Even your teeth bite your—"

"Tongue once in a while. Yeah, I know the fuckin' saying." Dallas turned his head toward the car.

"We gotta look after our own, Dally." Benny hawked up phlegm and spit onto the gravel. It shone like a diamond.

Wesley shook his head. "Wait, you two actually know each other? Oh this is rich. This is *real* fuckin' rich. Well I hate to break up the interracial romance but—"

Benny leveled the sawed-off shotgun at the officer. "Shut your mouth and toss your piece."

Wesley's finger tightened on the trigger of his pistol. He blinked at the old man on the scooter. "I don't think so."

Benny's grandsons raised their pistols in front of them, sideways and stupid like the thugs in rap videos.

"Put all your goddamn pieces down." Benny's voice held a fine razor edge to it.

"Gramps?" It was dick scratcher who asked the question.

"Put 'em down, I said. Don't need your goddamn help on this. Just got you two out of some shit, don't need no more right now."

The men did as their grandfather said, tucking their pistols in the waist of their saggy jeans.

Benny laughed and leaned back into his seat. "Now listen up, Officer Cracker. You throw that piece on the ground or you're gonna be nothin' but a splash of deadass on the side of your car that used to carry a badge." He pulled back the double hammers on the shotgun. "Toss the piece."

"You. Dumb. Dark. Son of a bitch." Wesley hissed through gritted teeth. "In about five minutes this whole fuckin' place is gonna be swarming with—"

"Shut your dumb ass lyin' mouth. If that was gonna happen, it already would have." Benny coughed and shook his head. "I'm willing to bet my dick and a dollar your CO doesn't even know your skinny white ass is out here tonight, you all wantin' to be Charles Bronson and shit. Be the hero, right? Save the world and all that hippie shit. Take your peace beads and shove 'em up your ass."

Benny wheezed. "I ain't telling you again. Drop the fucking gun or you get an extra fucking mouth in your belly." Benny smiled and his teeth were bright in the darkness.

Wesley pulled his gun away from Dallas and tossed it on the ground. "You let this motherfucker go and I swear to you, I'll bury you and your grandsons in a fucking ditch somewhere."

Benny raised the shotgun. "You out here all alone, ain't that right, Weasel? Somethin' happen to you, it'd be quite some time before anybody knew anythin' about it. There might be wolves out here, bears. Bet both of them love pork."

Benny coughed again, thumping his chest with a fist. "Dally? In my years of wisdom, I think it's in your best interest you get the fuck on up outta here and don't look back."

Dallas gripped the side of the car and pulled himself up. He turned to Benny and grinned. "We take care of our own, huh?"

"You know how it is." Benny smiled and motioned with the barrel of the shotgun to go on. Dallas started toward town, and broke into a run. Benny's cough came back again and hard. His body heaved on itself as he swung the barrels toward Wesley again and pulled the trigger.

The sound was an atom bomb detonating in the valley and the noise echoed off the hillside around them. Wesley slammed against the side of the car, the side of his right arm was whole one instant, a mass of mangled tissue in the next. The side windows of the cruiser shattered and fell like fresh-cut diamonds to the gravel. Blood and skin turned the door panel into a work of modern art.

Wesley screamed and ran around the side of his car, heading into the high grass of the fields behind.

"Don't just stand there playin' with your dicks. After him!" Benny bellowed.

CHAPTER FIFTY ONE

Dallas was hunched over and stumbling along Byron road. His lungs were screaming and his heart was performing a Neil Peart caliber solo in his chest. "I need a cigarette."

He stopped, put his hands on his knees and spat. Sweat trailed along his spine and he looked toward the line of trees he left the Kid in. *Better be doing exactly as I said, Kid.*

Dallas tried to get more air into his lungs, stood up, and kept moving. No choice. He snaked an arm around and rubbed the spot where the cop had been gouging him with that gun. Tomorrow, a bruise would live there. He suspected he'd have quite the collection of them come morning.

He looked over his shoulder once more and ducked off the side of the road into the woods.

Dallas lightly began to hum the lyrics Sam the Sham and the Pharoahs *Li'l Red Riding Hood* in his head. The Kid probably knew the names of the damned high schools the entire band went to and their life stories.

Goddammit, Kid.

Within fifteen minutes, Dallas saw his own porch light. More welcoming than any sun.

CHAPTER FIFTY TWO

The Kid had waited long enough. He heard some shouts and some tromping in the brush nearby but that was ages ago. He sat up and leaned against the log, wiping away all the leaves and forest debris from his arms and body. His stomach hurt, an unhealthy equation of hunger and guilt. He did his best to ignore it. He slowly started to make his way to the tree line, picking his footsteps carefully.

Stepping out into the open space of the high grass field, he saw several yards down, an SUV with the headlights on and the doors hanging open. Across from it sat a blue sedan. The Kid bent a little and took a few tentative steps in that direction. He could see the passenger side windows were blown out and there was something black splattered all over the door. He looked to his right and saw flashlight beams bouncing off in the distant woods. Faraway shouts.

The Kid screamed when he felt a hand grip his ankle and yank him down into the grass. The scream was quick and winked out like dying starlight.

CHAPTER FIFTY THREE

Victoria was working through her second bottle of wine. Through the course of the night, she had mingled the wine with a few healthy bumps of scotch and almost a whole pack of cigarettes. She also managed to eat a pear and some saltines in there somewhere.

Anger and vice were the closest of siblings. She chewed the inside of her mouth, trying to decide and eventually the alcohol made her choice for her. Victoria picked up her phone and hit Chad's number. It rang until she got the stupid recording about this number currently does not have a voicemail account set up.

Who the fuck has their own business but isn't smart enough to set up fucking voicemail?

She threw the phone across the room where it landed on the carpet by the bookcase. She had been aiming for the fireplace. She drained the last of her glass and stood up a little too quickly, teetering before regaining her balance and walking to the kitchen. She had just filled a fresh glass with water when she heard the knocking at the door—hard and frantic.

"This can only be good news, right?" She gave a bitter smile and sighed as she noted the clock on the microwave read 11:22 pm. She set her glass on the counter, tightened the belt on her silk robe and went to answer the door.

CHAPTER FIFTY FOUR

Dallas slung the door open to the trailer and ran inside. The chain at the top of the screen door screeched like a buzzard seeing fresh road kill. It was no Taj Mahal, but there were no neighbors for a mile in every direction and it was quiet. He was going to miss this place.

Shit, I'm gonna miss this town. This sad little dried up flyspeck peckerwood town.

"Goddammit, Kid." He spoke the words through gritted teeth and stood in the living room, took a deep breath and let it out slowly, waiting for his heart rate to settle down.

What the fuck did you get mixed up in? Who was that son of a bitch you were dealin' with? And the cop? The fucking cop?

He shook his head, trying to work out the angles here. *Was it the Musseys? Second thoughts on things? How the fuck did this go down? And Benny, you beautiful bastard, thank you. But how are you tied into this shit, too?*

Dallas had heard the shotgun blast behind him as he ran. It was something, but didn't mean much. There was no way to be sure if the cop was dead or alive, not that it mattered. He still had to get gone. Dallas had been doing this a long time and the Musseys going soft was the most logical thing. He'd been called off in the past once or twice because of second thoughts. He grabbed the neck of a lukewarm bottle of Budweiser on the coffee table and took a swallow. *But those jobs were only called off–the fucking cops weren't called in.* He took another long breath and exhaled. No use putting off the inevitable.

Best be gettin' on with it. Dallas walked the hall to his bedroom, grabbed a case and hurriedly threw some clothes inside. A couple pairs of jeans and several shirts. He reached beneath his chest of drawers and pulled out his pistol—a 1911 Kimber—and two extra magazines. He hated guns. Hated the feel of them and more so, what they stood for. *They were a statue to blind power and fear. Stony but cowardly gods best not to be bowed to. They were a soulless device.* It had been several years since he had even shot the damned thing, but he kept it oiled and maintained. *Y' never know.*

Dallas stuck the pistol in his waistline in the back, tightly beneath his belt, and stuffed the extra magazines in his jeans pocket. He looked around the bedroom. Not much else important.

Not important enough. Dallas walked to the living room again and paused.

When you get right down to it, deciding what's important enough to take, everything around you is... shit. Doesn't mean a damned thing. His mind reeled at what might be in the place. Documents with his name on it, things they might be able to track him with.

"Goddammit." He hefted the suitcase from the trailer, popped the trunk on his car and tossed it inside, then grabbed a handful of mud and smeared it thickly over the license plate. Not much, but it might help. Dallas walked to the rear and grabbed the snake tongs, then took the entire cage to the car trunk as well. The remaining rattler was pissy at being hungry and alone, the thing sounded like pebbles in a tin can. He put it in the car trunk and closed it up.

Walking to the back porch, Dallas grabbed the half-empty bottle of Cutty Sark he had left there yesterday, and stepped inside the trailer again. He spun the cap off with his thumb and took a pull, feeling the familiar burn against his tongue and throat, then upended the bottle and poured some on the sofa.

He pulled books from the shelves, watching *The Art of War* fall to the dirty carpet. *Grapes of Wrath. The Book of Five Rings. The Painted Bird.* Dallas splashed them all with the liquor and finished emptying the bottle as he sprayed the bottom edge of the living room curtains. He slung the bottle down the hallway toward his bedroom, then grabbed his pack of cigarettes from his jacket and lit one up. The smoke tasted heavenly with the adrenaline.

The chessboard lay on the coffee table and he noticed the Kid had made a move with his knight earlier. Dallas studied the board and slid his queen from its position, locking the Kid's king into place, pinning it with his own bishop.

"Checkmate, Kid."

Dallas flicked his lighter against the bottom edge of the curtains and flame erupted, jumping from one curtain to the next. Thick plumes of smoke curled from the fabric, and fire reached toward the ceiling. He picked up a tattered copy of *A Wrinkle in Time* and scrunched the pages, lit it, then dropped it to the pile of other books.

A soft puff as they ignited as well, and the stink of burning scotch and aged paper hit his nose.

And the fires of salvation shall set you free.

He glanced at the coffee table and the electronic pad sitting there. He picked it up and woke it from sleep as the flames licked the interior of the living room. The pad's screen lit up and Dallas saw the green dot blinking on screen. The location.

"Goddammit!"

Dallas tossed the pad on the pile of burning books, adjusted the pistol at his back and walked out.

CHAPTER FIFTY FIVE

"Imma need you boys to go to the bank tomorrow, first thing in the morning. I mean, first fucking thing. A cold wind's blowing and we don't want no part of it. Clear out the deposit box in the bank and come on home. Your names are on the account. Time to be moving, but don't mean nothing. Drive on." Benny half sang the last part, knowing well that his grandson's wouldn't recognize the words of Johnny Cash. *Goddamn shame, that.*

"That greasy mothafucka slipped away from us. His damn blood trail even stopped!" Dick- Fiddler half shouted.

"Sorry, Gramps," the other one offered.

His grandsons stared at the ground with embarrassment, and Benny nodded. "I know ya are. Don't matter much though." Benny scanned the line of trees, watching for any kind of movement, but saw nothing. "You boys are clear, that's what matters. I knew we were gonna have to clear out soon as that son of a bitch came knockin."

Dally, I hope you get the fuck up outta here. I did what I could for ya. I hope we meet up again one day. You're one of the good ones.

He glanced at the corpse with a gunshot in his face, the flesh on his neck gray and ruined. Swollen. Then at the still serpent lying next to it. Benny shook his head and softly laughed.

"Fuckin' rattlesnakes." He eased the shotgun onto his lap. "Let's go, boys. No use being around here with this mess anymore. Let's git gone."

CHAPTER FIFTY SIX

Dallas had told him to stay quiet and the Kid bit down on his tongue hard enough to taste blood, killing the screams he wanted to let loose. His mind ran with current.

Mama! Leave me alone, Mama! I'm sorry!

The muddy hand grabbing at his ankle was joined by another, clutching at the shin of his other leg, climbing him. The Kid tried to step back, shake it loose but the fingers were like vice grips on his jeans.

The hands were muddy and the Kid could see the blood splattered on her from what he'd done, from how he had ended her. *Mama no!* He wanted to scream out loud at her. Beat her off of him but he didn't want to touch her, to wrap his fingers around her pale, loose flesh, stinking of death. The Kid tried to shake his legs away from her, but Mama only pulled him closer, climbing over him to be face-to-face and clamp a hand around his throat. The Kid grabbed at the hand, trying to peel the fingers away but it closed even tighter. He did try to scream then, silence be damned, but it was too late. He felt his bladder about to give way.

"I'll fucking kill you if you don't help me."

A man's voice, not his Mama's. The Kid choked and sputtered as the grip loosened slightly. The moonlight shone down and he saw the cop from that clusterfuck back at the road. His face was a stone carving of rage, painted in sweat and mud. "Take your fucking shirt off. Belt too."

The hand left his throat and the Kid sat up, taking deep breaths, sputtering. "Get that look off your face, I ain't gonna rape you fer chrissake." The moonlight shone down on the other man and the Kid saw he was shaking. The Kid rose to his knees and pulled his sweatshirt over his head. He unbuckled his belt and handed it over.

The wounded man shook his head. "No. You're gonna have to help me out here, fuckstick." His breath smelled like meat left in the sun. "Take the shirt and wrap it around my arm. Tie the fucker tight as hell. Then we're gonna tourniquet near the shoulder to see if we can keep me from dyin'."

The Kid did as he was instructed—wrapping the hooded sweatshirt as tight as he could and then pulling the drawstrings tighter and tying them. He took the belt and wrapped it around the man's arm. He paused before threading it through the buckle and the man snarled.

"You run away or try anything and I'll kill you and everyone you love, you hear me? I'll blow their fucking brains out and you will goddamn watch me do it. I'll save you for last." The Kid pulled the belt with all his might and the cop hissed through chattering teeth.

The man's eyes rolled up to all white, and then they snapped back in place like doll eyes. The Kid let go of the belt and stood up.

The man grabbed the boy's leg and hoisted himself to standing. He took a moment to find his feet and glared at the Kid. "I fuckin' meant what I said. Remember it. Let's move."

The Kid only had two real family members alive–his sister and his uncle Skeeter–but he didn't think of either one of them right then. Instead, his mind went to Dallas.

CHAPTER FIFTY SEVEN

Victoria opened the door and saw Consuela standing there. She looked a lot different in street clothes instead of her maid uniform—faded jeans and a cute dark blue blouse—like a college girl on her downtime.

"Mrs. Mussey? We need to talk."

They sat in the living room, drinking a fresh bottle of wine and chatting like old girlfriends, but the topic of conversation wasn't old boyfriends and neighborhood drama. Consuela had heard Morris on the phone recently—an odd phone call. A call that wouldn't make any sense at all to most people.

Except Consuela's sister-in-law had a big mouth and knew things. Things normal people wouldn't know unless they were married to someone who worked at the Knuckle Bucket.

Victoria had heard of the place before. Chad had mentioned it to her a few times, but it wasn't exactly the place to go out for a Friday happy hour. It was a sanctuary for lowlifes.

Consuela had heard Morris mention Dallas on the phone.

"Mrs. Mussey..." Consuela leaned forward on the sofa. She picked up her glass of wine and took a sip. "This man, Dallas, he is a man who..." She glanced down at the table and then back to Victoria, meeting her eyes. "He takes care of people, you understand?"

Victoria cleared her throat, reached for the bottle of wine and filled her glass. *Oh yes, I know exactly what you mean.* She nodded at the woman and sighed.

"Consuela, it's late. You should get home to your son." Victoria stood, keeping a hand on the arm of the couch for balance. Part of her wanted to hug the woman, but instead she gave her another curt nod. "Wait a moment." She walked to the kitchen and opened her purse, grabbing her wallet and pulling cash free. Two, four, six. She folded the cash in her hand and walked to the living room again. "I'm not sure if you should come around for the next couple of weeks."

Consuela's expression dropped and Victoria noticed it. "Honey, you're not being fired. You're not in any trouble. It's just that..." She didn't know what she was trying to say. "There will be some things... some sorting out around here and it might not be the safest." She extended the cash to the woman. "Take this, and thank you."

The other woman hesitated. "I didn't tell you because I wanted money, Mrs. Mussey. I told you—"

"Doesn't matter, hon. I believe you, but it doesn't matter. Take it. You need to take care of your boy. And yourself. I have your number."

Consuela looked at the cash in her hand and reached out to take it. She pocketed the money and stepped forward, hugging Victoria. "You take care of yourself, too."

Victoria saw the woman to the door and locked it behind her.

The wine beckoned.

Her own conversation with Dallas came flooding back to Victoria. The nervousness she had on that call, along with the realization the man on the other end was speaking in code about murdering her husband.

"Morris, you son of a bitch." She drank two big swallows of wine and felt the sloppy, stupid grin rise on her face. "I didn't think you had it in you."

She thrummed her fingertips on the armrest of the sofa. What to do now? It comes down to money, I suppose. Whatever Morris paid Dallas, I'll offer more to call it off. It'll mean a little less after he's dead but I can live with that. *Live with that.* The double meaning of her words hit her and Victoria's smile grew wider.

Some games you shouldn't play, Morris. Not with me.

CHAPTER FIFTY EIGHT

Dallas pulled into the Swill-N-Fill and parked at the gas pumps. He all but ran inside and threw his money at the pimpled young man behind the register. "Twenty on pump four."

"Okeedoke. Was you at a fire?"

Dallas paused before he got what the fellow meant. "Trying to get some brush burned off before the next storm rolls though."

"Just in time. Calling for a beaut in a few hours."

Dallas nodded. He was nearly out the door when he stopped and turned to the cooler beside the entrance. He sighed and opened it. "This too." He pulled out a fiver and laid it on the counter. "Keep the change." He grabbed the bottle of root beer and hustled back to the car.

"Kid, I hope you're alright." He mumbled to himself as he stood and filled the belly of the beast with unleaded. He heard a vehicle coming down the road and knelt to make it look like he was checking his tire. He looked up and noted Benny's SUV hauling ass toward town. Dallas fought the urge to stand up and flag it down. *They were square. Even Steven.* He owed his life to that fat bastard.

The handle of the pump *thunked* announcing the tank had hit the pre-paid amount. Dallas yanked the nozzle free and put it back in place. Before he got in the car and started the engine, he heard the snake in the trunk. That bitch was not happy.

152

Chapter Fifty Nine

The building was cocooned in darkness save for one window near the back.

Morris Mussey was at the office. Sitting at his desk, staring at the spread of paperwork arranged for effect over the blotter. He took another swig of bourbon and sat the empty glass back on the desk. He looked at the picture of his wife in the pewter frame. She was in a sundress, standing with the sun behind her, it silhouetted her taut body. *A most fuckable body in profile.*

"Definitely gonna miss that ass," he slurred, and picked up the picture to bring it closer to the desk lamp. "And those tits. Nipples like strawberry gumdrops." He started to chuckle and was about to reach for the bottle on the window ledge when he heard a pounding on the door. From its ferocity he expected to see the glow of torches and the elongated shadows of pitchforks through the window. He sighed heavily and rose.

"This had better be a goddamned emergenc..."

His sentence ended abruptly when he pulled the door open.

Chapter Sixty

Victoria watched the bloodshot eyes of Consuela's taillights head down the driveway and let the curtains fall back in place. She felt the warm buzz of the alcohol.

Morris, you son of a bitch. She turned the thought over in her mind once more.

She paced to the kitchen, considered pouring herself a new glass of... something. Anything. She stood in front of the fridge and chewed the inside of her cheek for a moment, then turned and went for her purse instead. The clock on the microwave read 12:43. Morris still wasn't back from his meeting.

Meeting, my ass. Who's got their legs spread open for you this time? Who's lucky enough for your angry inch tonight? She spat on the floor and it was bright with blood. She sneered.

Victoria retrieved her phone from the carpet where she had thrown it earlier. No missed calls from Chad. There was a slight twinge of want in her head, a desire for a lost toy, but she ignored it.

He's up to some shit too, that cop, remember?

People lose toys all the time. They just get new ones. There are more important things to focus on at the moment. Much more important things.

Victoria thumbed through her recent calls until she found the number she was looking for, took a breath and leaned against the kitchen counter.

CHAPTER SIXTY ONE

I hate waiting. I fuckin' hate it. Dallas, what are you doing?

Dallas knew the smart play was to cut and run. Leave this town behind. The Kid. Everything. That was the smart play. He reached for his pack of cigarettes and found it empty, crumpled the pack and tossed it behind him in the rear seat, then reached for a fresh pack from his glove box.

His phone buzzed in his pocket and he pulled it free to check the number calling in. It seemed to register in his dust-covered brain but not familiar enough to answer, so he ignored it. He had to consider everything was compromised now. The buzzing stopped and moments later, the phone registered a voicemail. Dallas pushed to listen and a voice as smooth as salted caramel was in his ears.

"Uh, yes, hello. I booked... a vacation recently to Dallas. It seems there was some confusion and my husband apparently made the same arrangements. Must have slipped your mind to let me know, but I assure you, it's not a problem. Business is business, after all."

There were sounds of something shuffling in the background. Also clinking, ice and crystal—she was drinking.

"I'd like to cancel my husband's travel arrangements and upgrade my original vacation plans to avoid any accidental double-bookings. Whatever the cost is to upgrade, please do let me know."

The voicemail ended and Dallas put his phone down in the center console.

Mrs. Mussey knows. But how? Somebody fuckin' talked and that's not good. NONE of this is fucking good.

Dallas reached for the keys in the ignition. Time to get gone. He started to turn the key but stopped. The windshield was fogged from his breath and the heat he was giving off. Sweat poured from him in rivulets.

There is some shit going down. I've been doing this too long to not see it. But what the hell is it?

He packed the new pack of cigarettes and lit a fresh Winston, taking a long drag and resting his head against the seat. Dallas followed that first hit with another, and then one more. He rolled down the window and sat a few moments, watching the fog on the windows fade as the temps evened out. He nestled the cigarette between his index and second finger and held his arm out the window.

Dallas let his eyes close to think.

"You must show no pity. Life for life, eye for eye, tooth for tooth, hand for hand, and foot for foot."

Dallas sat in the front row, watching the sermon. The pastor held his worn and well-used copy of the Bible over his head as he preached.

Dallas picked at a thread in his dress pants. Part of him wanted to pull the thread but he also knew it would unravel the cloth and make things worse. It annoyed him, but also drew him, like an itchy scab on a healing wound. He flicked the loose thread and pinched it between his fingertips.

Mama grabbed his chin and forced his head up to focus on the Pastor. Her grip was tight and she shook his chin slightly for emphasis. Pay attention. "This is God's word. This is His justice. His law. Yes, we shall love one another but let not someone strike thee down lest they be struck." He paused, scanning the congregation, taking in faces individually. "An eye for an eye, sayeth the Lord."

The fireball between his fingers pulled Dallas free from sleep and he flinched, dropping the Winston, almost burned to the filter, to the ground. A trucker's alarm clock, as he'd heard the technique called in the past. Sometimes painful, but damned effective. He coughed and spat something thick out the window.

It would be easy to cut and run. Maybe head somewhere with palm trees or somewhere all four seasons actually meant something. Canadian winters were too fuckin' cold and he hadn't kept up very well on his Spanish, so Mexico was out.

Dallas punched the passenger seat.

No. It wouldn't be easy to cut and run. I don't like loose ends. Plus, people fucked with me and that won't do. I can't let that go.

Victoria knows Morris put a hit on her, but she's trying to buy her way out. Didn't call off the contract on her husband though. That was never part of the voicemail. So there was some wiggle room there perhaps.

The Kid. Goddammit, what is he mixed up in? I gotta get him loose of it and back home safe. And then there's whatever the fuck he is... the heat, what was he? Cop? Fed? Some Rent-A-Badge security fuck with tiny pecker syndrome? Why and how is that motherfucker involved at all? Is he alive or did Benny and his boys take him out?

And finally we have Mr. Mussey. I haven't been paying much attention to you lately and that's my fault entirely. What have you been up to?

Dallas pinched the loose thread in his mind and began to unravel it. After a while, the strained expression on his face eased, and then some more, until the creases on his brow almost entirely smoothed out. The beginnings of a smile on his face. He heard the noise from the trunk. Hail on a tin barn roof. His smile ripened.

Dallas turned the ignition over and hit the road.

CHAPTER SIXTY TWO

The pair looked like something from a horror film—one where a group is chased through the night by a family of jabbering machete-wielding maniacs. Mussey frowned as recognition of the smaller man dawned on him. The young man was slathered in dirt and sweat, his arms smeared with gore and mud. It was that kid that hung with Dallas. Mussey looked to the other fellow. He was at least a foot taller and twice the size of the Kid. His right arm was wrapped in a dark sweatshirt and was dripping blood. It looked like an enormous leech attached to his side. The man's color was awful—he was carved from gray soap.

Mussey started to speak when the bigger man put up his left hand. It held a gun.

"I'd say it's a bit of a fuckin' emergency, yeah."

Mussey looked at the Kid again, hoped like hell he could pass off as ignorant of who he was. He felt beads of sweat pop out in his forehead. Mussey took a step back toward his office. "I can call for an ambulance, just be a..."

"Stop right where you are, unless you wanna extra blowhole in your gut. I'm tired and as I'm sure you've sleuthed, my fucking arm hurts like hell. A million hells. I'm also a bit cranky and will not be tolerant of any horseshit." Wesley stopped and gulped air. He winced and his gun hand shook but he held it tight and kept it on Mussey. "Let's all go back there and have us a little sit down, 'kay?"

Mussey nodded and the trio made their way back to the office. Mussey sat behind his desk and the other two men sat on the sofa that abutted the far wall. The Kid looked ready to jump out of his skin. His leg was shaking like an overworked piston. Mussey sat and stared at the other men. "I'm sure this is some sort of..."

"Shut it." Wesley barked.

He looked at the Kid and nodded to his injured arm and the Kid grimaced and then grasped the wad of sweatshirt with both hands and squeezed it. Blood pattered to the floor like some sort of biblical rain. The elation that spread across the older man's face was unsettling.

The Kid repeated the action again and then wiped his hands on his ruined jeans. "Thanks," the gun-holder said. "Blood never seems as heavy when it's inside you, y' know?" He gave a soft chuckle.

"Mr. Mussey, I have it on good authority you hired a man to kill your wife. I also know for a goddamn fact the man who was fucking your wife—a man that is not you—hired someone to kill you." He let the words loose to buzz around the room like angry hornets. He sighed a heavy breath.

"So the wife-fucker wants you dead and you want your wife dead. Through a series of... extraordinary events, truly wild to be sure, wife-fucker is dead. You are not and the Missus... well, we ain't 100% on that are we? I'm here to get you and we'll go find out."

"I don't have any idea what you—"

160

"Stop. If you finish the lie your tongue just started stitchin', I will pull it out of your fucking mouth and use it to wipe my ass. All I said was fact. *Infuckingdisputable* fact. Now, you and he and me... we're going to check on your wife." The cop raised the barrel of the gun toward him.

"Where's Dallas?" Mussey looked to the Kid and the Kid turned away.

"I don't know. Ask the cop." The Kid spoke in a voice that was a cracked dish held together with cheap glue.

"You're police?"

"*The* police, fuckface. Capital fucking T on The." He waved Mussey out of his seat motioned for him and the Kid to move toward the door. They made their way to Morris's car. "Let's get to it."

The office door hung open like a dead man's maw.

CHAPTER SIXTY THREE

The junkyard was creepier this time. The rain had given birth to fog that slithered around the carcasses of the rusted automobiles and reflected the beam of his flashlight through the cracked windshields in spider web shadows.

Dallas skulked through the darkness, trying not to be reminded of the scene in *The Omen* where Thorn and the photographer are in the graveyard. Dallas kept his eyes peeled and tried to keep count of the rows he passed. Something darted in front of him and he stopped quickly, his hand reaching around for the gun nestled above his ass.

He flicked the beam towards the movement and saw the ass end of an opossum disappear under a rusted husk of a Subaru. "Hurry on home, Mama."

Dallas kept walking, albeit a little bit faster.

CHAPTER SIXTY FOUR

Victoria managed to stay in her lane—remarkable considering the copious amounts of booze she had consumed all night. *If I get stopped and have to take a Breathalyzer, I'll ring the goddamn bells like a winning slot machine.*

She smiled at the thought and turned into the plaza. She made her way around the side and stopped along the curb. There was a light on in Morris's office and the front door hung wide open. Victoria slowly got out of her car and made her way to the door, taking care with each uneven step. She looked down and noted the trails of dark droplets on the cement, following them into the office.

Flipping the ceiling light on, Victoria gasped when she saw all the blood in front of the sofa and the dark smears staining the furniture itself. Several footprints wove in and around the mess, ending beside the front door where it looked like the person or persons wiped their shoes on the carpet—deep red smudges ground into the pile.

Victoria savored the gruesome scene for a moment and then walked back to her car. She got in and lit a cigarette, after failing several times to meet flame to the tip. "Dallas, you dog. I see a five-star fucking Yelp in your future."

She took a drag from her cigarette and pulled out of the lot. Victoria headed home, careful to keep hands on the wheel at ten and two.

CHAPTER SIXTY FIVE

Wesley sat in the back seat behind the Kid, who was driving, slowly.

"You ever drive before, son?" Wesley sneered when he said it.

"No. I mean, I know how. I've watched people drive and paid close attention." The Kid's voice was halting and nervous. Morris was in the front passenger seat, shifting in place like a junkie needing a fix.

The sweatshirt tied around Wesley's arm was soaked again and the adrenaline was starting to wear off. It felt like a million stinging hornets had attacked him with stingers made of molten lead. In a way, he was glad it had been dark in the woods when the Kid had tied on the sweatshirt. He hadn't been able to clearly see the carnage done to his arm, but he was certain his bicep and the ligaments were nothing but tangled yarn and butchered meat. He could flex his fingers and hand but even the act of trying to raise his arm was a parade of agony. Still, Wesley fought through it, resting his gun hand against his knee, aiming at the back of the driver's seat. Wouldn't take much more blood loss before shit got really bad and that pissed him off more than anything. The weight of the soggy sweatshirt felt like it was sloughing the meat off the bone of his injured arm. This was going to need a better patch-up job and soon. He leaned heavily against the car door, positioning the bundled arm between his body and the car and leaned heavily. The pain was unparalleled but the blood ran down the grey vinyl in a sheet.

When this is over, I'm gonna find that old spade motherfucker and his grandsons and nail them to the fucking wall. You won't have to worry about going to prison when I catch you, and I will fucking catch you.

Wesley felt a fresh cascade of rage flow through him at the thought. His mind seemed to be sharpening. Focus coming back to roost.

Good. I'll run on nothing but anger right now if I have to, but this shit will be done tonight.

"Up here on the left. The one with the lights at the end of the drive." Morris pointed ahead of them and Wesley leaned forward. Beautiful house. Stone front with landscaping that was right off the pages of *Architectural Digest.*

"Well, well. Quite a little shack you got here, Morris. What's the matter, you didn't want to share with the wife anymore?"

Morris glanced at him but remained quiet. He turned away completely, looking out the passenger side window.

The Kid pulled into the driveway and put the car in park. The house was dark except for a dim glow coming from two windows on the first floor. The driveway itself was empty.

"The wife usually out this late?"

"I don't know what the hell she does with her free time. She's probably out spreading her legs or chugging a dick somewhere."

Despite the pain in his arm, Wesley grinned. "You talk so classy.

Well, we both know it's not the handyman tonight, don't we? Not unless she's got a thing for necrophilia."

Morris shook his head and reached for the door handle. Wesley raised his gun. "Don't even think about getting out of this car yet. You're staying with me." He leaned closer to the driver's seat and pressed his gun to the back of the Kid's head. "You. You're going to go in there and take a look around, see if the Missus is happily crocheting a new scarf, knuckling her snatch, or if her pretty brain's splattered all over the walls." Wesley pressed the barrel harder against the Kid's skull. "Clear?"

"Crystal." The boy had almost no voice at all.

"And I'll remind you... you run, try to run... even fucking *think* about running. You try to use a phone, pull any stupid shit at all, and I will skin Dallas alive while you watch. I'll use a carpet knife to take him down piece by piece until he's nothing but bones a dog wouldn't chew on. I'll keep him alive long enough to feed each of you one of his balls and then I'll kill you both... probably slow as molasses and make sure no one ever finds your bodies."

Wesley heard the boy give a soft cough, as if he was holding back tears.

Good. Be scared, you twitchy little fucker.

The Kid popped the door latch and stepped free, whispering to himself but not quite. "A is for Adam Ant. B is for ..."

CHAPTER SIXTY SIX

Dallas killed his headlights and brought the car to a stop about half a football field from the house. He slunk down in the driver's seat and rested his pistol in his lap. From here, he could see the front of Mussey's mini-mansion. Empty driveway but that didn't count for anything right now. He glanced at the backpack on the passenger seat and trained his eyes back to the house.

That little road flare of danger in the back of his mind threatened to spark up again and he tamped it down. No way he could leave the loose ends. No way he could leave the Kid. Everyone that boy had ever known had done their best to screw him up except his sister, who treated him like a leper, and his uncle Skeeter, who was so hopped up on meth lately, it didn't matter. It was a miracle the Knuckle Bucket was still open, but Dallas figured it was Henry and Darlene that pretty much ran the place anyway.

No, I can't leave the Kid, but damn this is bad.

A glare of headlights in the driver's side mirror caught his attention and Dallas slid farther down the seat. The car passed by and turned into the Mussey's driveway, and then stopped. At least two silhouettes in the car, maybe a third.

After a few moments, the driver's side door opened and Dallas watched the Kid step free of the car. His mouth was moving and his hands were clenching and unclenching in that dying pigeon impression he had, and he walked to the front door and went inside.

The fuck're you doin' Kid? Why are you here?

Dallas looked back at the car. Two figures remained inside. Dallas leaned into his passenger seat as another set of headlights flared up behind him. He watched as Mrs. Mussey's car moved past him and paused at the end of the driveway. She waited a bit, and then eased forward behind her husband's car.

He pulled the slide on his 1911 to make sure a round was chambered. Dallas got out of the car and tucked it into the front of his waistband.

CHAPTER SIXTY SEVEN

Victoria turned up the volume on the car stereo, letting the loud music vibrate through her. She thrummed her hands on the steering wheel and hum-sang to the bass line of Heart's *Barracuda*.

The deed is done.

For the first time in a long time, she felt free. Light. A thousand pounds gone from her shoulders.

I'm happy as a clam right now. Victoria laughed out loud at the phrase. *But why are clams happy? I mean, are they? Really? Loose as a goose? I don't think so. Haven't screwed that many men. I'm not loose. Happy as a pig in shit? I guess, but that's a little... disgraceful. Happy as a clam, it is. And my clam will be even happier when I'm surrounded by palm trees and tanned cabana boys bringing me tall drinks. Not to mention spending all that money.*

She steered the car onto her street and yawned, the buzz of alcohol fading and giving way to the pull of a satisfied sleepiness. Victoria reached the end of the driveway and hit the brakes.

What the fuck is Morris' car doing here? Fucking Christ, I didn't see his dead body. Is this part of it? Did Dallas bring the car here? Fuck, Dallas! Did you even get my voicemail?

Victoria chewed the inside of her cheek, tasting blood again. She

eased her foot off the brake and pulled into the drive. Inside Morris'
parked car, a figure with a bloody face turned in the rear seat to look
at her.

The bloody face was smiling.

CHAPTER SIXTY EIGHT

Dallas crept along the side of the car and hunker-ran over the hedge that aligned with the sidewalk, keeping low and alert the entire time. He paused at the end of the driveway, staying hidden behind the brick monument bearing the house number.

"No matter how much money you got, still ain't nothing but a number," he muttered as he knelt and peeked between the landscaped shrubbery. Mrs. Mussey had parked but was still in her car. He could hear muffled music coming from it. Heart.

Not a fan but oh, the things I'd have shown those sisters.

Morris' car was still there. There was someone in the back and he could see a vague silhouette in the front passenger side as well. The person in back turned their head and smiled in the direction of Mrs. Mussey.

The fucking cop.

Dallas felt his gorge rise and swallowed it back down. It tasted like nicotine and bile. He flexed his hand holding the gun and looked off to the side of the drive. It was wooded and offered the best cover, so he slowly made his way into its shadowy arms. He crawled on all fours to get as close to Mrs. Mussey's car as he could. A large cloud rolled over the moon and killed the feeble light, keeping him cloaked in darkness, and for that he was thankful.

CHAPTER SIXTY NINE

"Ma'am." The Kid's voice was a dying sigh in an old folks home. He swallowed spit and tried once more. "Um. Miss Mussey?"

He scanned the room and noted they had a large collection of books, mostly historical fiction and a few horror novels. He memorized the names and titles and kept scanning. Large television. Laptop on the sofa. Expensive decor and crystal. He made his way to the kitchen and saw empty wine bottles on the counter. Glasses in the sink, all rimmed with lipstick smudges. The Kid wanted to stop what he was doing and wash them.

He kept looking around and his gaze fell upon a wooden block next to the toaster. A wooden block that sprouted knife handles like porcupine quills. He looked over his shoulder and slowly withdrew the largest of the knives. His hands were tacky with the blood of the cop and he fought the urge to scrub the mess free of his skin. The Kid turned and made his way upstairs.

He had just stepped into the master bedroom when he caught movement from the corner of his eye. Looking out the window, the Kid saw from that angle he could see the driveway—more accurately, part of it. Morris and the cop were obscured from his view by the roof of the garage, which meant they couldn't see him either. The Kid stood still and watched for the movement to repeat and it did.

Someone, or something, moved in the shadows under the trees. The Kid tightened his grip on the butcher knife and saw, in a flicker of moonlight, the man hiding beneath the cover of the trees. The Kid didn't bother to hide his tears or his smile. He turned and made his way back down the stairs in the empty house, sliding the knife into the rear waistband of his pants.

CHAPTER SEVENTY

Kid, I know damn well you saw me. Whatever you do, don't blow my cover. Just stay cool.

Dallas side-waddled over to where the trashcans were lined up. He knelt against one with a yellow lid and peered around it quickly. No one had gotten out of either car yet. The music had stopped in Victoria's, and aside from the slow rumble of the vehicles idling, it was quiet. Eerily so. He was about to creep closer to the garage when he heard a door open and saw the Kid step from the front of the house.

"She isn't here." The Kid shouted and waved to the men in Morris' car. The back car door opened first and the cop got out. He stood stooped to one side. His arm was wrapped with cloth.

"I know she ain't in there because she's right over there in her car!" Wesley hollered.

The cop's walkin' but Benny must have fucked him up pretty good. He looked like a wax effigy, he was so pale. The sheen of sweat made him look coated in glass. Just pass out, you son of a bitch.

The cop made his way around to the passenger side and opened the door. Using his gun to show the way, he guided Morris out of the car. "Up and out, no bullshit. As in zero."

Dallas watched everything very closely. *What the fuck is happening here?* He held his breath and didn't move a muscle. Somewhere in the woods, the crickets started up.

"Move it, Mussey. Go stand next to the kid over there. I'm going to collect the Missus." Wesley walked over to the front of Victoria's car and tapped the hood twice with his pistol. He smiled at her through the windshield and nodded for her to get out. She opened the door and got out.

Dallas felt his mouth go dry when he saw her, reminded of how beautiful she was.

"Whooowheee! The hell you wanna snuff a fine piece of tail like this for, man?" The cop barked at Morris out of the side of his mouth. "Ma'am, get on over there with your shitbag husband and that weird fucking kid. We're gonna go inside and have us a little meeting of the minds."

The cop walked behind the other three and Dallas saw the man's gaze was trained on the woman's ass in the confines of her thin dress. He couldn't blame him.

That is one mighty fine turdcutter.

CHAPTER SEVENTY ONE

"Be a peach and get me a dishtowel, would you? In fact, get me two. And a glass of the strongest liquor you've got." Wesley ordered as Victoria walked from the dining room into the adjoining kitchen, leaving them sitting at the polished cherry-wood table. "And turn on the stove and put on the biggest frying pan you got."

"You hungry?" Morris stammered and tried to smile.

"Not even a little." Wesley wiped the sweat from his forehead on his red-stained sleeve.

Wesley was a smear of wet dog shit. Sweat poured from him and in the glow of the overhead dining room chandelier, his skin bordered on the color of fresh spackling paste. The Kid's belt, cinched around the sweatshirt wrapped around his arm, had beads of blood on the worn black leather. He coughed and sniffed and stared at Morris and the Kid, sitting on the opposite side of the table.

Victoria came to the dining room and set a glass of amber liquid and two maroon-colored dishtowels in front of Wesley.

"Did you want that pan sprayed or buttered or anything? I got no idea what you plan on cooking."

He shook his head and waved to her with his pistol to sit on the other side. "No. It's fine for me." The smell of hot metal began to waft in from the adjoining room. Wesley grabbed the glass, raised it

176

to his mouth, and took a solid drink. "Johnnie Walker Blue?"

Morris nodded affirmation.

"Should have known." Wesley took another drink, set the glass down, and then pulled the belt strap tight, thumbing open the buckle one-handedly. He let the belt loop slide down to his elbow and hang, droplets of blood falling to the oak floor below. Gingerly, Wesley peeled the edge of the Kid's sweatshirt away from his arm. A tacky sound, like an overused Velcro wallet being peeled open came from the cloth and Wesley sucked in a breath through gritted teeth. He paused and then with much labor stood. "Let's go Morris." He paused and stared at the other two. "You and the Kid stay put. I'll be right over there."

"I can help if you want." The Kid said.

Wesley gripped the pistol and straightened it out. "I believe I said to stay right the fuck where you are, Kid." Wesley glared at him with bloodshot eyes, and continued unwrapping the bloody cloth. It fell to the floor with a sloppy wet-mop sound and Wesley groaned and shook his head. Even the feeling of the wound being exposed to open air was electric pain coursing through him.

He tried not to focus on what the wound itself looked like, but it was hard not to. The tissue beneath was an overripe tomato burst open from being in the sun too long. Shreds of his flesh reached from the underside like jellyfish tentacles.

"Morris, steady me and get us by the stove." The smaller man did as he was instructed. Wesley sucked in a deep breath and spoke: "I'm going to take that pan and sear this fucking wound closed. You try anything—*anyfuckingthing at all*—and I will melt your face from your skull with it. Got it?"

Morris had gone cataract white and his lip trembled. "Um... sure."

"Here we go." Wesley grabbed the handle of the pan and touched the bottom—a twelve-inch disc of heated tempered steel—to the bottom half of the mess that was his arm. It hissed and sizzled as the meat and blood cooked to melted flesh almost instantaneously. The kitchen filled with a smell not unlike steaks grilling. Wesley hissed through his teeth and shakily put the pan back on the burner to reheat a few seconds. The flames from the burner whispered over the bits of skin and blood on the bottom of the skillet.

Wesley screamed and shook his head, and then sighed heavily. His face glistened with sweat and he looked at Morris. "I smell pretty tasty, huh?" He smiled and Mussey looked like he was going to vomit.

"Okay, round two." Wesley repeated the procedure and then dropped the pan to the floor. His arm was like something from a nightmare—seared, blackened flesh and bright red scabs rimming it like jewels. All of the flesh surrounding the burned area was bright slapped-baby pink and swollen to volcanic peaks. Feathers of smoke were rising from it. Morris lost his steel and puked all over the counter.

Wesley cuffed him by the neck and steered him back into the dining area.

"C'mon, Princess."

Using the fresh dishtowels, Wesley draped one over his bicep.

He felt the liquor threaten to come back up from his stomach and gritted his teeth. He turned his gaze away, breathing in through his nose and out his mouth several times, and got himself leveled out again. Then he used the other piece of cloth to finish wrapping his arm. He raised the belt loop and began pulling it higher again, cinching it not any tighter than necessary to keep the terrycloth in place.

This is bad. The sensation made the muscles of his legs turn to water and the room tilted sideways, but Wesley flipped the buckle pin in place and he fell back against the chair with a heavy exhale.

"*Hoorah!* That was somethin', wouldn't you say, Morris?" Wesley bark-laughed and reached for his glass of Johnnie Walker. He threw back what was left and set it down harshly on the table. Morris stared at the tabletop as if hypnotized by the salt and pepper shakers at its center.

"All right then. Let's get down to brass tacks and sort some shit out." He didn't raise his entire arm, but Wesley used the barrel of his pistol to point at each of them as he spoke. "You have *allllll* been... bad. Little. Monkeys. So no bananas for you." He tittered at his hilarity.

CHAPTER SEVENTY TWO

Dallas could see the lights flick on the first floor as the four of them walked inside. Movement inside a room to the left of the front door and a little farther beyond.

No back up. No other cops or feds. No helicopter. What the fuck? He's either a dirty cop trying to pull a shakedown, or he's gone off the rails. Neither is good. So what now? They're too close to the front door for me to go all Chuck Norris and shit.

He kept low and made his way to the right side of the house, past the garage, and once he was out of their line of sight, Dallas walked quietly and quickly toward the rear of the building. A deck extended from the house and through the sliding glass doors, Dallas could see a soft glow from inside the house.

He made his way to the stairs leading to the deck and crept upward. The blinds weren't drawn on the sliding glass door and now he could see the light was coming from a room deeper inside the house.

Dallas gripped the handle to the sliding glass door and lifted upward slightly, easing the weight off the lower track, then pushed to the right to test the lock. The door was unlocked and it moved open with his action. Dallas continued inching the door along, slowly, until there was enough room for him to turn sideways and step inside. He found himself in the back half of the living room. Dallas stepped across the carpet and crouched down behind a loveseat. He wrinkled his nose, the entire place smelled like burnt meat and vomit. He grimaced and leaned against the wall to listen.

"–complete clusterfuck! But if you want a chance at getting out of this, you'll give me what I want. To be specific, *who* I want."

"I can... I can make a call and try to reach him again."

That was Morris Mussey's voice replying to that asshole cop. Dallas clenched his jaw.

He maneuvered to a crouch behind the loveseat, and from his vantage point, could see the top edge of the kitchen door. Dallas guessed they must be in what must be the dining room. He scanned the area for better cover and found none.

"Fuck yes! See now, that's what we call cooperation!" The cop's voice was harsh and out of focus, like a good ol' boy who had been drinking all day at the bar. "Like they taught ya on Sesame Street. Makes things happen! You two better learn from that, especially you, pretty boy. Oh, I know some people in prison who are just gonna *love* you."

Dallas held his left palm over the top of his pistol and used his right thumb to ease back the hammer. It clicked in place much louder than he thought and he braced for the rushed sound of movement. There was none.

"And you, hot pants, oh, there is going to be some serious Cell Block H porno shit going on when you get booked. By the end of your first night, your chin'll look like a glazed fucking donut."

"Fuck you."

"Fuck me? Seriously? *FUCK MEEE?* I think I might be the only dick in this room you ain't ridden!"

The sound of a chair being scraped violently along the floor and then falling came from the room.

Dallas walked around the sofa and put his back to the wall beside the dining room doorway.

"I'm finally starting to understand why you wanted to snuff her out, Morris. I'm really starting to get it, now! Fuckin' hell, I might just do it for nothin'!"

Dallas closed his eyes and took a breath.

Chapter Seventy Three

Victoria felt disgust at the fact her stomach was growling, no doubt spurred to such action by the smell of Wesley's cooked arm.

I could totally eat a steak.

Her mouth filled with saliva and she hated herself at that moment.

She looked out into the darkened living room area. The moonlight through the bay window offered a thin fang of silvery light. She had almost started to zone out on the darkness in there when a quick movement caught her attention. Wesley was still fiddling with his belt/towel contraption. Morris was blankly staring at the table and the Kid was all darting eyes and shaking leg. She took her gaze back to the doorway leading to the kitchen and living room. She flinched at first, and then tried not to smile when she noticed a shadow on the wall holding the silhouette of a gun.

"Is anyone else hungry?" She asked, sliding back her chair and putting her hands atop the table's surface. The men all stopped and looked at her.

"I haven't eaten since breakfast. And I've not been running around working up an appetite getting shot or kidnapping people... so *you two* must be starving." She started to stand and Wesley leveled the gun her way.

"What the hell do you think you're doing, Donna Reed?"

"I said I was hungry. I thought I would go make some sandwiches or something. Shit, a box of fucking Wheat Thins would do the trick at the moment." She stared at him and did not return to her seat. The next few moments rolled by tensely.

"I like mustard on mine." Wesley finally said, "And remember, no bullshit or God as my witness I will shoot every single one of you and fuck the holes!" Victoria stepped away from the table and made her way into the kitchen. They heard cupboards opening and the quiet hum when the fridge door opened.

"Fuck, Morris. That chick's got balls so big, you're practically gay!" Wesley's laugh was as moist as fresh road kill and didn't smell much better.

CHAPTER SEVENTY FOUR

I'm gonna make you proud of me, Dallas.

The Kid knew his mind was trip-firing, fuse-blowing fast at the moment. Every single detail around him seemed like it was too sharp. He could smell Wesley's cologne. The soft-as-a-mouse-fart *tick-tick-tick* of the rich man's wristwatch. The cop's breathing, haggard and rough, as if each inhale was snagging on something as he drew in air. Smell of wet pennies, of the blood on his wounds, and the sweet fried meat odor of his burned flesh. Even from the kitchen, the Kid's mind focused on the sounds Victoria was making—crinkling of cellophane packages of meat and cheese. The sound and pulse of his own thumping heart in his ears.

The cop rested his wounded arm on the tabletop and the pistol in his hand tilted sideways as his hand, if not his grip, relaxed.

The Kid looked at the kitchen, at Victoria, and the cop's gaze followed. As he did, the Kid smoothly reached for his waistband and gripped the handle of the knife, slipping it free. His leg wanted to shake free of its moorings but he willed it to be still even though he was absolutely buzzing inside.

I caused this. It's my mess. I'll fix it, Dallas. I'll fix it.

CHAPTER SEVENTY FIVE

It happened as gently and as wildly as the first kiss of summer love. Like boiling thunderheads ushering in a storm of torrential proportions.

Dallas spun around the edge of the doorframe and trained his pistol on the cop. Textbook perfection for a man who hated guns.

And like every tender kiss of young passion, every bruised sky of lightning and chaos, the initial beauty and innocence comes to a violent flash-fire end.

Dallas had the cop dead to rights, but pulled his aim because of the Kid.

The Kid jolted upright, the chair he sat on flung away from his body, and he leaped across the table. He plunged his right hand down toward the cop, showing the flashing silver blade of a butcher knife in his grip. Wesley held up his injured arm in a reflexive defense and the blade cleanly removed his middle and ring fingers at the second knuckles. They fell wriggling to the table like great pale worms.

The knife's descent continued, and its point sunk, dead center, into the meat just below the wrist of the man's good arm. The blade gave a dull thud as it sliced through Wesley's hand and into the dining room table. The cop's fingers flexed open like the legs of a stuck crab. His face was a mask of terror. His mouth was open but no sound fled from it.

The entire scene happened like a lightning strike, the actions burned to Dallas' retinas and then gone in an instant.

But by then, Dallas had already pulled the trigger.

CHAPTER SEVENTY SIX

Dallas's gunshot missed the mark, but caused Wesley to jump and his finger clenched on the trigger of the pistol. A second loud bang and then Morris was making a face like a fish trying to cough up a hook. The front of his polo shirt blossomed red flowers, spreading like gruesome Kudzu. There was a dark spot at the tip of his breastbone, about four inches south of his Adam's apple. It was black and angry and spewing crimson rage down the man's chest. Morris tried to rise but stumbled backward, taking the chair with him.

Wesley swung his now blood-slick pistol in his wounded hand and the butt connected with the young man's forehead with a loud crack. The kid's eyes stopped darting and rolled over white as he fell to the floor.

Wesley turned and swung the pistol at the handle of the butcher knife, knocking it loose of the dining room table. He bit the tip of the handle between his teeth and ripped his hand free of the blade, and then his mouth gaped open, dropping the knife to the carpet. He howled as blood from his drizzled the Kid's face. The pistol fell from his damaged hand to the table, creating psychedelic spin art with his blood.

Victoria screamed and ran from the kitchen to kneel by her

fallen husband. She held his clammy head in her lap and leaned over his face. He was whispering to her and she nodded. Dallas stood frozen in place, his gun aimed at the cop who was busily untying the belt from his arm and wrapping it around his wrist. His pistol lay on the table in front of him.

Wesley leveled a look at the man that was apocalyptically dire. Dallas stepped forward, his pistol trained on the cop. He contemplated blowing the man's head off then and there but he needed to get the Kid out of here and with the amount of blood the cop was losing he wouldn't last long. Dallas picked up the Kid and leaned him over his shoulder, and then beat feet back down the steps and out the door.

CHAPTER SEVENTY SEVEN

Wesley growled as he cinched the belt through the buckle and yanked it with his teeth. He looked down at the woman on the floor, with the dying man in her lap. He shambled to the stove and turned the burner back on.

"Seem to forget that not two hours ago you were willing to pay that motherfucker to kill this asshole for you. Now you're all *Steel Magnolias* tearfest over him?"

Wesley picked up the pistol in his good hand, well–good in that it had all five digits–and walked back to the stove. He stopped and looked back over his shoulder.

"You're in it now, whatever comes of this... at you, is yours, read me?" Wesley stood and watched her a moment longer before he thrust the stumps of his missing fingers into the ring of gas flames, a sizzle filled the pocket of silence around them. Smoke rose from the burning flesh and Wesley shook in place. His jaw clenched and his face reddened as he held his breath and his lips moved with the pain. He jerked his hand away from the flame and screamed into the kitchen. Taking deep, gaping breaths, he slowed his exhales down and stood straight, staring at Mrs. Mussey.

Her face was shining with tears and snot. Victoria nodded and began to wail again.

"Fuckin' slits!" Wesley turned the burner off and began fanning the hand to put out the small flames that tipped the charred stumps of his missing fingers like vile candles. He closed his eyes and sniffed in the air, shook his head and stared at Victoria, his eyes bulging.

"Be well," he said and winked at her before descending the short set of steps. He headed through the living room and toward the front door.

As soon as the door slammed, Victoria stopped sobbing. She wiped her face on her arm and stood up abruptly, her husband's head loudly *thunking* off the floor.

"Sorry, Doll." She smiled and grabbed her keys from the counter. Morris blinked and opened his mouth to speak, but instead of words, thick pink foam bubbled from his lips, followed by stillness. She pooched out her lower lip in a pouting gesture and walked to the entryway.

Victoria went downstairs and almost as soon as the door slammed the third time, Morris gave up the ghost.

Chapter Seventy Eight

Dallas had managed to book it out of the house and get to the car in record time. "Not bad for a chain-smoking geezer."

He congratulated himself as he hoisted the Kid into the passenger seat. He ran around and got in his own side and was putting it in reverse when he saw the large shadow exit the house. He watched the hunched way the figure moved, and deduced it was Officer *Givemeafuckingbreak.*

He slammed the car into drive and put the hammer down. Tires squealed and the car took off down the darkened street. The Kid had slid down so much his knees rested against the dashboard. Dallas tried to pull him up with one arm but he was too heavy, which struck him funny given how thin the boy was.

"Stick with me, Kid. You need to make it through this so I can kick your ass." He laughed and it was a manic thing.

Dallas kept his speed up as he chewed the winding road out of town. He licked his lips and realized he had no cigarettes. This shit just kept getting worse. He pushed his foot to the floor.

Chapter Seventy Nine

Wesley couldn't hold onto the wheel very well. It was slick with blood and he couldn't get a decent grip on it. His shoes were sticky, and he heard the gummy sounds as he switched from brake to gas pedal.

"I'm gonna get you... both of you fucks."

Wesley ground his teeth and played out scenarios as he drove well above the speed limit. He favored the one where he caught up to Dallas and shot him right in the dick and left him to bleed out while he took the Kid apart piece by piece.

It's gone too far now. No way this can end within the confines of the legal system. I've taken too many sloppy liberties.

Godammit! All I wanted was the big collar and the glory, maybe some spit on my dick and a nice raise. Fucking respect. What do I get? Shot and knifed and made fool of...

Wesley was coming up on a split in the road. He saw signs about the bridge being condemned, but he turned in that direction anyway. He had a hunch and it felt fucking right.

CHAPTER EIGHTY

"At the Copa! Copacabana!"

Victoria didn't even have the car stereo on. Didn't even *like* Manilow but she was still belting out the lyrics with the windows wide open and the wind raking her hair around her face. Off key was an understatement. Islands and hot spots and plunging neckline bathing suits were on her mind. That, and margarita lagoons brimming with cabana boys she could play with, tire of, and replenish.

It hadn't gone as planned, that was certain, but, for whatever reason, in his final moments, Morris had found whatever love and empathy he had for her once upon a time.

Oh my God. His final words, his dying words, were for me. To help me. If I still had some semblance of a heart, I'd be outright fucking touched.

Her laughter fluttered out the open window and into the night like hysterical bats.

CHAPTER EIGHTY ONE

Dallas killed the headlights of the car but kept the running lights on as he approached the silhouette of the bridge. Sign after sign had announced it was condemned on the mile stretch of back road.

But what did that really mean? Some county inspector decided the supports had a few pieces of concrete missing? Enough of an issue to grease the palms of some contractor on county payroll to get an overpaid state project for six months?

He pulled the car to the edge of the bridge and stopped. It was an old steel structure, rusted beams branching overhead with steel planking along its length. Probably a place the local teens came to jump off into the river during the high heat of August.

Dallas stared into the rearview mirror. He hoped the cop wouldn't second-guess things. The fork in the road a mile back led to this condemned bridge or straight onward to hit the highway—the smart choice for any criminal.

Or a very, very dumb one. Once someone hit the highway, air support could be called in. Highway patrol put on the lookout for make, model, and color. Dallas thought the cop was way off the reservation the way he was behaving. He was so far gone, Dallas doubted there would be any support at all brought in. In fact, Dallas thought the man was downright psychotic, but even crazy people can act sane once in a while.

CHAPTER EIGHTY TWO

The boy looks up into the sun-kissed face of his mother. The cigarette in the corner of her mouth hisses as she takes a drag, and smoke curls up into her squinting eye. Her fingers are busy knotting the rope around the boy's thin ankle.

"Ma?" The boy opens his mouth but an old man's voice trickles from it.

"Yes, son." She cocks her head like cute doggies do and stands up. There's dirt on her knees and he watches an ant slowly making its way up her thigh. He feels exactly like that ant. So very small.

"I'm in a mess, Ma."

"I know you are."

"Show me the way?"

"I tried once but you got loose and left me." She looks down at him and dank muddy water begins to pour from her mouth and the corners of her eyes like tears.

"I didn't mean to."

"I know, baby." She places a clammy hand on his cheeks and lightly pinches the flesh there. Suddenly, her face is very close to his. He can smell the low tide stink of her and see the minute wrinkles in her pale skin. She smiles and a minnow drops from a gap in her teeth.

"Sometimes, the way forward is to go back again."

He feels her hands on his chest and then he's falling again. The water is rushing up to wrap him in its churning embrace.

CHAPTER EIGHTY THREE

A groan from the passenger side yanks Dallas back to the present. He checks the rearview. A pair of headlights, still a fair distance away, rounded a curve on the road but were headed this way.

You motherfucker.

Dallas eased off the brakes and onto the bridge. The metal planking beneath the car shifted slightly in their anchor bolts but it held. He was torn between creeping across the structure and flat out gunning the car to make it across to the other side.

He glanced at the Kid in the passenger seat and then forward to freedom on the other side of the bridge. He swiveled his head, feeling his neck bones pop and gripped the steering wheel.

"Fuck it." Dallas slammed his foot onto the gas pedal and the rear tires spun gravel behind him in a rooster tail. They gave purchase and the car lurched forward onto the bridge.

For ten whole feet.

A 3x3 foot steel bridge panel on the driver's side slid sideways, shearing off the rusted bolts keeping it in place and Dallas felt the entire car fall, the frame itself shuddering onto the bridge platform and carry forward with momentum.

"FUCK!" Dallas slammed his fist onto the dashboard.

"FUCKIN' MOTHERFUCKER!"

He looked at the rearview mirror again and the headlights were gaining distance. Dallas killed the running lights and slapped the Kid as hard as he could on the side of his face. "C'mon Kid!

His eyes fluttered but didn't focus, and Dallas slapped him again. "Wake the fuck up, Kid!"

Dallas flung his door open and the lower edge scraped the metal planks, barely giving him enough space to crawl from the driver's seat. He pulled himself free and reached into the back for the knapsack on the floor. After he slung it over his shoulder, he went around the rear of the car to get to the passenger side. Jerking the door open, Dallas grabbed the collar of the Kid's jacket. "Kid, you need to snap out of it. We need to move. Now."

The sound of tires skidding to a stop on loose gravel came from his left and Dallas ignored the noise and the harsh glow of the lights. He pulled his pistol, holding it at his side and opened the rear passenger door, crouching behind it.

CHAPTER EIGHTY FOUR

Wesley was tired. Dead ass tired. A thing run over in the fucking road needing to be scraped up with a shovel kind of tired.

He stopped at the end of the bridge. His high beams illuminating the car stuck in the middle. He sat for a moment and watched the car. He breathed deeply of the abattoir stink that filled his vehicle. He killed his engine, picked up the pistol from his lap and opened the door. It squeaked loudly and that sound tore a rift in the almost silence of the night, its only competition at the moment being the whoosh of the river below.

Wesley could no longer feel his arms—not fully. They were leaden things that held too much weight. He looked at the pistol in the ruins of his right hand. His index finger on the trigger, he flexed it slightly to make sure he could seal the deal and it followed command, the action also caused the burnt scabs to crack and fresh blood to flow from the neighboring stumps. He sighed loudly and stepped out of the car.

In the distance, he saw Dallas scurry around the back of his hobbled automobile. He spat onto the dirt and started toward the center of the bridge. His headlights made his limping shadow look like a monster about to level Tokyo.

CHAPTER EIGHTY FIVE

Crouching below the door panel, Dallas let the backpack slide from his shoulder to the steel plates he stood on. He heard the gravel at the edge of the bridge crunching beneath the cop's feet, as he closed in—as slow and casual, as if he was going to the corner store to get an ice cold drink.

No. Not quite. There was a slight drag to the man's second step. He was hurt. Hurt badly.

He glanced at the Kid. Still nothing.

Goddammit, Kid.

Dallas swiveled on his foot and raised his pistol in the same motion, aiming it through the space between the rear door and the body of the car and firing two quick shots at the shadow marching toward him. His aim caught the driver's side headlight and as it blew out, Dallas ducked down again. There was no satisfying thud of meat falling to the gravel.

The window of the car door detonated as a bullet blew through it, raining glass tears onto the steel around Dallas. Another shot rang out close enough overhead to sound like an angry bumblebee.

"Dalllllllasss!" The cop yelled but the energy behind it was fading like sunlight at the end of a hard day's work.

He could hear the cop breathing hard, but he was still getting closer. *No way in hell I can wait him out 'til he just collapses.*

"Dallas... it was a good run. It really was. But it's over. So why don't you just—"

Two echoing booms and twin bullets punched through the car door beside Dallas. He saw the glow of headlight and smoke shining through. Five inches closer and it would have clipped his left shoulder.

Desperate times called for desperate measures and this was goddamned desperate. Dallas sighed. *Fuck it.*

He rose to his feet and pointed at the center mass of the cop. *Aim big, miss small.* Dallas fired off three rounds and winced as he felt a heated rush go past the left side of his face.

His third shot was true and a mist of liquid burst into the brightly lit space behind the man. Dallas saw the man's arm float back down to his side and the cop dropped to his knees and fell forward, face down onto the dirt and stone.

"Hey Dallas?"

He spun around, away from the dying cop and found the Kid standing beside the car, leaning on the hood with one hand and holding the other to the back of his head. He gave a gentle smile at Dallas in that soft crooked way of his.

Blood spilled over the Kid's lips and down his chin. The smile on the Kid's face turned to confusion and he stumbled against the car door and slid to the ground in a heap. Dallas noticed the dark wet spot where his hand had been on the right side of the back of his head. And the elated smile that he'd been wearing evaporated.

Chapter Eighty Six

"Kid? Kid!" Dallas tried his damnedest to remain calm. "*Nonononononono!*"

He held an arm under the Kid's slight shoulders and was holding his face with his other hand, long calloused thumb at the corner of his too red lips.

"Dallas?" The voice was brittle, an ancient nest made of paper and twigs.

"I'm here, son." Dallas felt like he was choking, something slimy and large was blocking his throat and he could neither breathe nor swallow.

"I think I got shot." The Kid half smiled but it disappeared as quick as a wish. He licked his pale lips and went on.

"I'm scared, Dallas. Don't let me die. I don't wanna see Mama again. Don't want her to come near me." His eyes began to leak tears, running pink across his skin in the glow of the headlight.

"Die? Shit, Kid. You're not gonna die. You're gonna be fine, you hear me? You take it easy now. You're gonna be okay. Close your eyes and rest, I'll get you home."

"Home with you?"

Dallas smiled and tasted his own tears. "It's the only one you have, son."

The Kid managed a feeble nod and closed his eyes. Dallas leaned in, less than an inch from his face, and started to whisper.

"Say it with me now. A is for America and B is for Bread..."

By the time he got to C, Dallas was sobbing. He gently lowered the Kid to the ground and smoothed his filthy hair from his eyes. He smiled at the Kid and it was the most full-of-love thing he had ever done.

Dallas stood and screamed at the world.

Chapter Eighty Seven

Dallas was listening to the last echoes of his rage boomeranging in the night when he heard movement behind him. He turned and his mouth opened slightly in disbelief.

"Fuck you, Dallas. That was like a TV Special it was so touching." The cop was on his knees, smiling through his slurred words.

Two shots rang out at the same time, sharing the same echo as the sound rolled across the black mercury surface of the river water below.

Dallas dropped the pistol to the steel surface of the bridge where it clattered through the girders and into the whooshing blackness.

The cop remained on his knees a moment longer, then fell forward to the dirt. The back of his head glistened with chunks of wet tissue in the glow of the remaining headlight.

"And fuck you right back, you son of a bitch."

Dallas turned and walked back to where the Kid was and stood for long minutes just staring at the boy.

Dallas picked up the Kid and carried him gently to the edge of the bridge. He cradled him on the railing, out over the water and looked again into those closed eyes. That face.

"To the waters and the wild... For the world's more full of

weeping than you can understand."

He let the boy go and kept his eyes squeezed shut until he heard the splash. He ducked under the bar that served as a rail and stood looking at the pale shape in the inky darkness below. Dallas held the railing with one hand and leaned farther out, watching the Kid float just beneath the surface, like a prize under glass.

"Do not be afraid of those who kill the body but cannot kill the soul. Rather, be afraid of the One who can destroy both soul and body in Hell."

Dallas watched the black mercury waters flow beneath him. He closed his eyes, let go of the cold railing of the bridge, and fell into the abyss.

CHAPTER EIGHTY EIGHT

Victoria smiled with her mouth and eyes when she saw the blue Ford Escape at the end of the row of vehicular carcasses. "Oh, Morris." She giggled as she walked over to it and opened the rear door. The reek of dampness and muck tickled her nose.

She looked in the rear and saw a backpack on the floor. It looked bigger than what her old man had told her and it wasn't blue but green. But the man *was* dying after all. She reached in and grabbed the backpack by the canvas strap on the top. Victoria smiled and slung it over her shoulder.

Did something move in this thing?

She quickly dismissed it and practically sprinted to her car. Victoria got in and turned on the light by the rearview mirror and sat the bag in her lap. She turned on the stereo and a blast of Foghat filled the car. She licked her lips and yanked open the zipper, pulling both sides of the bag open wide so she could see the money.

If the music weren't so loud she might have heard the muffled warning of the rattle.

WRITER BIOGRAPHIES

Robert Ford fills his days handling marketing and branding projects. He has run his own ad agency, done a lot of freelance, baled a lot of hay and forked a lot of manure.

And once had to deal with a *very* overripe iguana.

He has published the novels *The Compound*, and *No Lipstick in Avalon*, the novellas *Ring of Fire*, *The Last Firefly of Summer*, *Samson and Denial*, and *Bordertown*, as well as the short story collection *The God Beneath my Garden*.

He has co-authored the novella *Rattlesnake Kisses* with John Boden, and the novel *A Penny For Your Thoughts* with Matt Hayward.

In addition, he has several screenplays floating around in the ether of Hollywood.

He can confirm the grass actually is greener on the other side, but it's only because of the bodies buried there. You can find out what he's up to at his official site: robertfordauthor.com

John Boden lives a stones throw from Three Mile Island with his wonderful wife and sons. A baker by day, he spends his off time writing or watching old television shows. He likes Diet Pepsi and sports ferocious sideburns. He loves heavy metal and old country music. And shoofly pie.He's a pretty nice fella, honest.

His work has appeared in *Borderlands 6, Shock Totem, Splatterpunk, Lamplight, Blight Digest,* the John Skipp edited *Psychos* and others. His not-really-for-children children's book, *Dominoes* has been called a pretty cool thing. His other books, *Jedi Summer With the Magnetic Kid* and *Detritus In Love* are out and about. He recently released a novella with fellow author Chad Lutzke called *Out Behind the Barn.*

He has a slew of things on the horizon.

LAMPLIGHT VOLUME 1

lamplightmagazine.com/volume-1

This 450 page anthology of the first year of LampLight Magazine collects four amazing issues from September 2012 - June 2013.

Features the complete serial novella "And I Watered It With Tears" by Kevin Lucia. Fiction and interviews with Robert Ford, Kelli Owen, Ronald Malfi, and Elizabeth Massie.

J.F. Gonzalez takes us through the history of the genre with his Shadows in the Attic articles. LampLight classics bring you some of those past voices to experience again.

Fiction by William Meikle, Nathan Yocum, Rahul Kanakia, Ian Creasey, Mandy DeGeit, D.J. Cockburn, Christopher Fryer, Christopher Kelly, Tim Lieder, Jamie Lackey, Matthew Warner, Sheri White, Dinos Kellis, S. R. Mastrantone, Mjke Wood, Delbert R. Gardner, Michele Mixell, Sarah Rhett, Armel Dagorn, E. Catherine Tobler

LampLight Volume 3

lamplightmagazine.com/volume-3

The third Volume of
LampLight magazine, collected
into a single volume, featuring
issues from September 2014 -
June 2015

Featuring the full novella by
Kelli Owen, *Wilted Lilies*. Fiction
and interviews with Yvonne
Navarro, Mercedes M. Yardley,
Nate Southard, Victorya Chase.

Fiction from: Gary A.
Braunbeck, Sana Rafi, Nick
Mamatas, Roh Morgon, Tom Brennan, Salena Casha, Rati
Mehrotra, J. J. Green, Damien Angelica Walters, Gwendolyn Kiste,
John Boden, Kristi DeMeester, T. Fox Dunham, Davian Aw, John
Bowker, Kealan Patrick Burke

Made in the USA
Monee, IL
22 July 2020

36876700R00132